Ruth

TO FACE THE SUN

Newport was a typical New England Yankee town. The natives looked down on holiday-makers even though they spent part of each year in Newport.

John Leavitt was a native, and also a store-keeper with a very attractive daughter. When Frank Levinsky, one of the ' summer people ', started dating John's daughter, there was bound to be talk. But John was not as bigoted as some, so when the question came up of Meyer Levinsky, Frank's father, buying the old village cemetery at tax-sale to build a discothéque, John faced a good many people he'd known all his life—and opposed them.

The entire town was forced to sit up and take a long, hard look at itself. John Leavitt was vindicated, yet he felt very unheroic. There was no way, at that late date, to make amends for the town's early hostility—or was there?

To Face The Sun

by
JONI FROST

ROMANCE BOOK CLUB
119-121 Charing Cross Road
London W.C.2

PRINTED IN GREAT BRITAIN BY
BRISTOL TYPESETTING CO. LTD.
BARTON MANOR - ST. PHILIPS
BRISTOL 2

CONTENTS

CHAPTER ONE

Two Ways of Life

THERE WERE always social problems, if not small and local then national or international and huge, troublesome, even dangerous and explosive ones. It seemed to be part of the exorbitant cost people paid for living in a communal atmosphere. And yet, if they did *not* live as social animals with all the orderly processes of orderly animals, then, of course, a good many of them would perish.

But—and this was Jerrie's mood—would it be such a frightful thing if most of them *did* perish? Junior Walton, for example, the town drunk, or Jonah Sutherland, who'd been a thief since early boyhood and now went about big and surly, with two prison terms behind him, or Emil Franzen, the bigoted, disagreeable farmer at the edge of town who took great delight in being an obstructionist?

In fact, if the entire town of Newport were obliterated tomorrow, aside from scattered relations across the nation of those who became defunct, who would really be hurt or dismayed? No one, actually. Newport was a holiday village along the New England coastline with the oily Kanaki River beside it. It flourished in the sticky, muggy summertime, resplendent with boats and gaudily dressed holidaymakers, most of whom owned cottages on the outskirts or along the Kanaki River. In wintertime Newport became a cold-bound village huddled close to its stoves with so little business being transacted that except perhaps for the grocery store everyone else might as well not exist anyway.

The setting was excellent. Northward and north-westerly were soft-blurred stairstep mountains clothed year round in the bluish darkness of spruce. Excepting July and August there were very few insufferably hot days, and even in those months there was usually a good cooling breeze about sundown which persevered until bedtime.

And regardless of the heat one could always cool off. There was the ocean—which no one bathed in—and of course there was the broad and turgid Kanaki River, favourite swimming area in many a mile.

Newport itself had once been one of those lovely New England villages, nostalgic even for those whose roots did not trace back to New England, with quaint homes, immaculate little clapboard churches, brick stores and green lawns. It could have at one time been used as the basis for a work in oil entitled *Typical New England Village*.

No one had ever made that painting and now no one ever would. The ' summer people ' as the natives referred to the holidaymakers, had wrought a subtle change. There were six taverns, a movie house specialising—during the summer at any rate—in Italian pictures, a huge log roadhouse where people danced all night to live music, and all the fringe businesses which sprang up, like toadstools in a forest, where city people congregated. There was the One-Stop Loan Company next door to old Henry Sherman's saw-sharpening shop, the Smiling Frankie Bigsky haberdashery—Quality On Easy Terms —and Little Abe's Used Cars—Guaranteed Like New —Nothing Down, Your Own Terms.

The Episcopal church had closed its doors two years earlier; attendance had dropped so drastically it was impossible to maintain the building let alone the minister. Now, there was talk the place might be sold to a general contractor named Levinsky who, or so it was said, proposed to re-model it into a discothéque; a place for bearded, sandalled, wanderers to hold their sit-ins and love-ins and sniff-ins.

But degradation, as the local people saw it, was reached in earnest the day Jennie came home with the story—
" purest gossip " she called it—that Newport was going to have the privilege of a Presidential visit. For as long as anyone could remember, Newport, like all rock-bound New England, had cherished Republican ideals. The President, who probably hadn't got ten registered votes in the entire community, was a Democrat. It was unthinkable that he'd visit Newport, unless, of course, it was because the rude and noisy and flamboyant 'summer people', most of whom simply *had* to be Democrats, were somehow arranging this to irritate the natives.

The evening newspaper, *The Newport Herald & Monitor*, referred to simply as " the *Herald* ", offered a more subtle suggestion. In editorial acid it said that very probably the President was coming to Newport because,

A*

at least during the summer, there were many more Democratic than Republicans on the local landscape.

Such a statement caused a great collective groan to arise from native throats. Any number of grass-roots prophets emerged to say "I told you so," elaborating on this theme so heavily that each point, well made or not, became supper-table conversation in Proper Newport, which meant Native Newport.

But of course it was all too little and too late. For those whose candour matched their honesty there was always the truthful fact to face up to that when the 'summer people', had first begun coming, Newporters couldn't do enough. Those with stores had extended credit, those without stores had become dealers in cabin sites, those with the most to lose were so busy plunging hands into strange pockets they were blind to the very future they were encouraging.

A few knowledgeable and unruffled natives simply said, "You asked for it. A blind man could have seen what you were doing, but no, as long as they came like sheep to be fleeced, you were in there shearing with both hands. Well; now make yourselves a nice woolly blanket and sleep in it!"

True or not—and of course it *was* true—candour and the facts didn't alter anything; there were simply too many 'summer people' parading around; the women—in too-tight capri pants, or in nose-bleed-like Bermuda shorts—dropping litter, poking fun at locals, sneering at customs and traditions which had survived from Revolutionary times.

The men were largely over-fed, smoked constantly, drank immoderately, and while less open in their criticisms of natives—they were vulnerable, the women were not—nonetheless had their little snide remarks to make when a quick reconnaissance indicated no one was at hand to take them up.

On the whole, though, both classes got along reasonably well, but then these were affluent times; no one had the energy for serious trouble, nor the inclination either, when the stomach was full, the weather pleasant, the bills paid, and another month of vacationing lay ahead, or, as someone said in Leavitt's Emporium, Newport's old-time general store heavily patronised by natives. " The best time to wage a war or snipe at the neighbours is when both sides are so fat and lazy the whole thing's done from under a shade tree in a hammock."

There was discrimination but on a subtle scale; natives patronised their long-established business establishments and shunned the newer, gaudier places. Picnics on Sunday never included ' summer people '. On the other hand the roadhouse, the Italian-oriented cinema, the hire-purchase stores, were heavily patronised by newcomers. A newcomer being anyone who had not been in Newport or at least New England since the era of Thirteen Colonies.

There was possibly less of this division among the small children who attended the local schools than among their elders. In this case ' elders ' including the secondary school children—teenagers—or college ' men ' and women '.

Old Caleb Adams, whose pedigree met every stringent demand of blue-nose New Englanders, being something of an outlaw because he said Thoreau was all tommyrot, further heightened the distaste of his fellow villagers by maintaining stoutly that if native folk didn't like ' summer people ' for the asinine clothes they affected or their boisterousness, or perhaps even for their thoughtlessness in having French, German, Italian parents, it proved once again that bigotry in New England was little different now than it had been during the witch-burning days, and that a people whose own forefathers had fled Europe to found their Federal Union because of discrimination and persecution in other places, could be excused less because they should know more.

Caleb also said disliking a whole gaggle of people, most of whom one had never personally talked with, was as utterly psychopathic as disliking all cats because one scratched you as a child, or disliking all birds because one let fly with pinpoint accuracy on your Sunday finest on the way to church.

Naturally no one heeded Caleb Adams. Despite an illustrious New England lineage he lived on a weedy strip of inherited acreage along the Kanaki River and did little more than fish or set lobster traps. He'd never married, never worked for others, at least as far as anyone could recall now—Caleb being somewhere in his seventies by his own admission—and had only taken orders once, also by his own admission, and that had been during World War I.

It was partly old Caleb's fault Jerrie was in her savage mood that pleasant, dazzling afternoon when her mother arrived home from a bridge game to begin preparing dinner. Jerrie had been talking to the old man. Some of his free-thinking had rubbed off as it frequently did with Newport's upcoming generation.

For one thing Jerrie had been away to college for three semesters and was currently at home because of a recent appendectomy. Missing classes doubtless made her fretful. Missing other things, including the heady social whirl, also added to her sense of loss and chagrin. Her father had said she was feeling sorry for herself, which was his usual way; he liked to capsule everything, make it easily understood and thereby readily dismissible.

But Jerrie's mother was a round, full woman with laughter in her grey eyes and a world of understanding in her heart. She also happened to be quite pretty and in fact twenty years earlier had been without question the belle of Newport. To those who still wondered why she'd married Jerrie's father proper New Englanders had one irrefutable reply: Because he had breeding and good prospects.

Jerrie resembled them both. She had her mother's fine softness. The eyes were smoky grey, the mouth full and rich and generous, the nose straight and proud, the figure full and sturdy and muscular. She also had her father's quiet thoughtfulness and at times his cold-rising steady temper. She never ' exploded ' in anger. When either Jerrie or her father got mad it was a slow-kindling, steady growth of practical, uncompromising wrath.

In other times Jerrie would have matured, married, had her children in the Newport General Hospital, and perhaps have died and been buried all within the accepted limitations of New England's traditions and comfortable customs, but as things now stood she could not do most of those things and she knew it, which was what added to the fretfulness of her mood this day.

Her mother recognised the storm signals and, using inherent and age-old mother-wisdom, swept into the house with only one cheery greeting, leaving Jerrie to sit out there under the ancient poplar in the rear yard with her unutterably profound dilemmas, which at nineteen were beyond any doubt totally beyond resolving by man and perhaps even by God as well.

CHAPTER TWO

The Leavitts

MEYER LEVINSKY told John Leavitt in the latter's barn-like general merchandise establishment on Main Street that if the Selectmen approved his application to re-model the old Episcopalian church into a discothéque he'd begin work immediately, and, providing John could meet the competition, Meyer would buy locally.

John Leavitt was Jerrie's father. He was as tall as Meyer Levinsky—an even six feet—and perhaps twenty or thirty pounds lighter, but where Meyer wore a good deal of his weight out front in a formidable belly, John wore his weight evenly distributed and well proportioned.

He had no illusions about either Meyer Levinsky or his purpose in visiting the Newport Emporium—General Merchandise At Fair Prices. John was one of Newport's Selectmen—town councillors anywhere else—and Levinsky was fully aware of that. Further, by confiding in Leavitt Levinsky wasn't exactly offering a bribe but he was making it plain enough that if this permit were approved Leavitt would profit therefrom.

John was polite. " There will be opposition, Mister Levinsky."

" Oh sure," said the city-man airily. " Ain't there always opposition; sore-heads, reactionaries, old fogies?"

John's face coloured a faint red. " There are enough coffee houses already."

Levinsky's pale blue eyes came to rest on John's smooth but square-jawed Yankee face. " Coffee houses? Mister Leavitt, there ain't a single coffee house in Newport. All right; cafés you got, even a roadhouse. Some beer halls too. But no discothéques. Look; maybe you don't know what a discothéque is, Mister Leavitt. Ask your kid. She can explain what a discothéque is. And take my word for it, Mister Leavitt, kids are coming on in Newport like everywhere else. They deserve a place strictly their own."

John nodded as a customer walked past, watched to be sure one of his clerks moved in, then turned back to Meyer Levinsky and said, " The Episcopalian church has been a landmark in Newport for over a hundred years, Mister Levinsky. Most of us were baptised there."

" All right," shot back the builder. " But no more." Levinsky thought a moment, his round heavy face devoid of discernible expression. " Look, Mister Leavitt; when I was a kid my folk always went to the same synagogue. You know what? It's gone now and who remembers it— or the rabbis? Don't misunderstand me, Mister Leavitt; a kid should learn to believe in things. But ever since

I can remember your kind and my kind been moving farther and farther away from the old ways. Listen; I got two sons, Meyer and Frank. They never ever been inside a synagogue. All right; my father—he should rest in peace—used to eat me out about that. How do you explain to an ailing old man things have changed? You don't. So I took the hard words and kept silent. You understand?"

" I'm afraid not."

Levinsky went thoughtful again, then said, " Statistics tell us there are as many kids in America today as older people. Well; they got their own ways, their own world."

" Hippies, Mister Levinsky, beatniks?"

" Naw. You know better. Those fugitives from a cake of soap get the publicity but they're a small minority. I'm talking of the kids like your girl and my boys—the ones who want to know things. They're the future, Mister Leavitt, just like you and I were the future twenty-thirty years back. Only now there's so damned many more of them. So—we called it a soda fountain in our day and now they got this foreign name—discothéque. So all right, they drink coffee instead of sodas. It's the same. They're smarter'n we were, Mister Leavitt; they're searching. Us? We fooled around with old cars and went to the movies. Times change, ideas change, *kids change*. I'm sorry the old church don't pull in its congregation any more. In that respect you and I are alike. I'm sad for what used to be and isn't any more. But what's the sense in crying or wringing one's hands? No sense, so we look ahead. Mister Leavitt; let 'em have their discothéque."

John said, " There are two other Selectmen, Mister Levinsky."

Meyer nodded slowly, making a quiet appraisal, then he said, " Sure. Well; I just wanted to get it off my chest. Win, lose or draw, I had to do that much."

After he'd gone John returned to the high stool in the office where he'd been working on Accounts Receivable; it was close to the end of the month and the bills had to be ready for mailing on the first. But he kept wondering about Meyer Levinsky. Not about the discothéque; that had already been turned down in every Selectman's mind before the application had come in. The old Episcopalian church was historic, it was part of a time John Leavitt and all the other natives cherished and mourned. What he wondered about was the boyhood of a Meyer Levinsky. About his parents. About his schooling and his principles. One thing he'd said was becoming increasingly clear: Times were changing, had changed. But the facts of human existence being basically conservative, the older John got the less he liked change. He didn't actively oppose it but like all his generation he turned a cold shoulder to it, forestalling in all the little ways its progress.

But Levinsky had been straightforward. Except for that hint about buying through the store if the application were approved, Levinsky had made hard sense. One of the clerks came in and asked about a customer's credit. John straightened on the stool to gaze out into the cavernous store where the customer stood, then nodded and the clerk departed, looking relieved. The old man out there was Caleb Adams. He was slow, always, but he paid.

John smiled softly to himself. Caleb had been one of John's father's customers fifty years earlier when the store had passed to the father from John's grandfather. Caleb was a cantankerous old free-thinker; that's what John's father had snortingly called him. Well; old John Leavitt was long gone but there stood indestructible Caleb Adams, reputedly descended from two Presidents of the United States—a slow payer but dependable.

Georgia arrived before noon, as she often did, to make her husband take her to lunch at the one decent café in town. Watching her come up the oiled floor towards his office John thought of her as he always had; a beautiful girl although now forty, with a look in her blue-steel eyes that made his heart beat a little faster. It was odd but undeniably true that some men, usually strong ones, only had one real love in their lives. Folks called her Madge.

Georgia Leavitt was of all things, related to old Caleb Adams. It was a distant and devious relationship which was not unusual in small-town New England, and except for the elderly people who put store by such things was scarcely ever mentioned.

It had been snidely said by some of the more scornful ' summer people ' that this was precisely what had diluted the blood and strength of New England; everybody was related to everybody else. It was one of those comments that didn't make any real sense but there were always people willing to repeat them.

Georgia shot a glance at the old Seth Thomas clock in the gloomy old office and wrinkled her nose as she often did at the smell of the store, which was compounded of many odours, but most noticeable in summertime was the resinous scent given off by the oiled fir flooring. John hadn't once oiled the floor since inheriting the family business but both his father and grandfather had consistently done so once each year, and now that cumulative dousing stubbornly lingered both in the colour of the very dark old planking, and in the smell. It wasn't objectionable, exactly, but it certainly dated the place.

"Luncheon," said Georgia, gazing past her husband to the ledgers. "Where is Emily?"

Emily Trotten was the book-keeper. Had been for thirty years. She was a short, plump spinster with decided ideas about everything, and was that rarest of all a man's acquisitions, a book-keeper who knew the background of every customer. She never allowed the store to lose money if she could help it, which entailed little personal notes on most past-due statements which somehow always seemed to achieve their desired ends such as: 'Let it go this month, Edward; I see in the papers the price of lobsters are down again."

"Shopping," said John. "She wanted the day off."

Georgia considered the cardboard box her husband was using for the statements and said, "I'll come back and help this afternoon."

He went after his coat. "No need. It hasn't been that big a month. Anyway, I never mind making out the bills. How's Jerrie today?"

"Better. Not the itching scar from the appendectomy, the spirit."

He nodded, shouldered into the coat and said, "Meyer Levinsky, that builder from the city, was in a while back about the old church."

"What's that got to do with Jerrie?"

"He talked quite a bit. It was mostly about kids nowadays. He's got those two sons you know."

"Yes, I know. Meyer Junior and Frank. I heard

this morning the army is calling up Meyer."

John looked up. " Is that so?"

Georgia held the door and afterwards quietly closed it. The door was one of those half-glass old-fashioned panels with black lettering on it: *Office—Newport Emporium—J. Leavitt & Son.* John's father'd had it installed but neither his son nor his son's wife ever fully understood why; the place for a business establishment's name was out front, not deep inside on an office door.

It was hot out but there was a little breeze in off the ocean. It had the ocean smell too, a concoction compounded of dead fish, ancient seaweed, salt water and paint. There was always someone down along the docks and wharves painting boats. In fact two chandlers did a brisk summertime business down there refitting and outfitting.

Newport's main thoroughfare was nearly half again as long as it had been when John and Georgia had been youngsters. All these additions were products of the trade resulting from increased ' summer people '.

The locals patronised a restaurant called Rosie's Café; a neat, clean, no-foolishness little establishment, sandwiched between two old business houses. It wasn't gaudy by any standards and the tables still had cotton plaid tablecloths instead of murkily designed shiny Formica or plastic. Also, the waterglasses were of that slightly barrel-shaped very heavy glass one rarely saw any more. The food was good, plain and well cooked. Rosie herself was a portly, ageing woman with the build of a woodsman. Her dead husband had been a small, dark man from Canada. She had dominated him like she dominated many of her customers.

She no longer waited table but sat on a high stool at the cash drawer deploying her waitresses like troops and keeping tight hold on everything that happened. She smiled seldom and frowned often. Rosie was a hard-headed businesswoman in her late fifties.

She smiled though when John and Georgia Leavitt entered. Smiled and waved in fact, but then she'd known both since they'd been children and had been one of the most truculent defenders of their plighted troth.

As they eased into the wall-table John said, " One thing Levinsky said that I hadn't thought too much about, was that people just aren't as religious now as they were."

" And he had a solution?"

" No," said John, gazing at his wife. " Madge, don't be antagonistic. Levinsky—well—he may not belong and all that, but I can't shake the notion he's more like us than we are like him."

Georgia's slaty-eyes grew speculative. " I'm not antagonistic towards the man for what he is, John, only for what he wants to do. We were married in that church."

John ordered for them both, handed the waitress back the menu and gazed around. It was early and most of the other patrons of Rosie's Café hadn't arrived yet.

" Why doesn't he leave the old church alone, John, and just build his café or whatever it is on some of the vacant ground?"

The answer to that was very simple. " What vacant ground, love? Newport's grown out past the church. It used to be beyond town, remember? Look at the town now, then think back to what it used to be. Before too long they'll be gobbling up the last river frontage. And there hasn't been any ocean frontage in five years now."

" He could still build his own place, couldn't he?"

" Yes, but the church would be an ideal location."

" John, are you in favour of what he wants to do?"

" No. But I keep remembering some of the things he said."

Georgia eyed her husband, who was a good, quiet and fair man. " Mister Levinsky must be quite a persuasive talker."

Their luncheon came and for a while neither of them spoke. By the time they were finished the café was filling up, so they greeted people and were greeted in turn by those they'd known all their lives, so nothing more was said about Meyer Levinsky or his projected discothéque.

CHAPTER THREE

Caleb Adams

FRANK LEVINSKY was odd in some ways. For example, although he had one of the fastest boats on the Kanaki River he never raced. For another, although he was known to be Jewish, he was fair and blue-eyed and tall, with a lithe leanness which went well with an almost off-hand, quiet-smiling personality. Even the natives said Frank Levinsky could have fitted in anywhere, meaning of course anywhere New Englanders gathered.

He was studious, pleasant, soft-spoken and serious. But once Jonah Sutherland, the town black-sheep, who was a hulking man, sneered when Frank and Jerrie Leavitt were eating at Rosie's, and before anyone really knew what had happened Frank had chopped Jonah down with the edges of his hands, a most unusual way to fight by all orthodox New England standards.

His brother Meyer was darker but nearly as tall as Frank. But Meyer, also good-natured, was louder and brasher. He was not obnoxious, actually, just full of brassy confidence and enthusiasm. When he was taken for the armed services he shrugged it off by saying when he came home again he'd own the army or whatever he ended up in. It was a pointless joke and didn't sit well with the locals who disapproved of any kind of brashness.

And Meyer drove his car fast. He didn't care for boats, so rarely went out in them, although at the Levinsky place on the river there were three at the spacious, immaculate, white-painted dock.

It was one of the ironies of Madge Levinsky's existence that their expensive and beautiful country property had to be contiguous with old Caleb Adams' hundred acres of brush-snarl, shade trees, warped and weathered ancient house facing the river from a gentle slope, and the sound of coughing ancient motors every morning when Caleb went off fishing in his scruffy old boat.

But Meyer's wife had to bear that cross, for, as her husband had once pointed out, " He was here first and, moreover, the old man's perfectly harmless. He'll die one of these days and whoever gets that hundred acres might even be worse. Madge; count your blessings."

Her retort had been sharp. " Meanwhile he depreciates the property value on all sides."

Meyer had got a little annoyed, saying exactly what had been in his mind when he'd first bought river frontage at Newport. " Listen; I didn't come up here from the city to speculate. I came here because the air's clean and kids shouldn't grow up without knowing how to use their hands—how to work on a motor, how to fish and hunt and swim and learn self-reliance. That old man suits me just fine."

What Meyer might have said if he'd seen Frank and Jerrie sitting in the shade of Caleb's huge trees round the old rickety house, talking with Adams, might not have been so tolerant, for Caleb could always be relied upon to have strange views. As he said often enough about himself, " When a man's lived too long with nothing to do but use his head, he comes up with some queer notions."

Those ' notions ' did not very often even come close to paralleling the convictions of Meyer Levinsky. Nor, for the matter of that, did they approximate the convictions of the natives. But if dissent had any value at all, at least as far as Newport was concerned, then old Caleb was a worthwhile citizen. The problem was, though, that not very many people, native or ' summer people ' believed this to be a fact.

It never bothered Caleb. " When I start agreeing with everyone else," he told Frank and Jerrie, " I'll start suspicioning myself of getting senile." He smiled widely, revealing worn but perfect, strong teeth. "That'll mean I'm getting old." He was already at least seventy, and could have been five years older by his own admission, for although his branch of the illustrious Adams family was just as prolific in ideas as the other, more famous branches, it had never been noted for its degree of fidelity respecting records, or for that matter, wealth.

"My daddy used to say a man could store up one kind of riches or another kind, but never both, and he chose to store up things about as I do. Memories, pleasures, laughs, jokes."

Frank Levinsky said, "Mister Adams; you could be a wealthy man. Just sell the hundred acres."

Caleb's faded grey eyes lingered on Frank. "Where would I go, son? I've lived here all my life. My folks lived here before me. And their folks. Anyway, at my age what do I need with a lot of money? Tell you what though; if it'd all been possible forty, fifty years ago, I still wouldn't have done it. I just told you son, a man can't acquire both kinds of wealth and my kind's never been your daddy's kind of riches."

The old man looked at Jerrie. He'd known her since babyhood exactly as he'd known her father and mother. "Geraldine; the longer you put off going back to school the more of an education you're going to get. Newport's changing fast, these days. By my reckoning, one more summer ought to see it."

"See what?" she asked.

"The war, child, the war." Old Caleb smiled at them both. "I remember my daddy telling about the Civil War when I was barely up to his knee. Most terrible thing, he said, that can ever happen to a man or a nation is to have your reasons for being in opposition rooted in your own soul."

Frank was eyeing Caleb strangely but Jerrie, sitting beside Frank on the old silvery bench under the trees, had no inkling what Caleb meant. The old man explained.

"It's been coming a long while. You must have suspected it. Now it's coming to a head. Frank, you know what I'm talking about?"

"Maybe. I think so."

"Name it, boy, name it!"

"Well; change. Turning the old church into a discothéque. Things like that. The 'summer people' versus the natives."

Caleb nodded, no longer smiling. "I was thinking only yesterday—where do you two fit in? Do you see what my daddy meant? Each of you belongs on different sides of the same fence. Jerrie; your folks don't want the old church made into a roadhouse, do they?"

"Not a roadhouse, Mister Adams," said Frank quietly, and fumbled the explanation badly. "A discothéque. A sort of meeting place for the disenfranchised—at least that's what some of them call themselves. Like a café only without much food." Frank trailed off into dumb silence.

Caleb waited, then said, "It doesn't make much difference what it's called, son. It's the idea. It's going to divide people right down the middle like my daddy said of the Civil War. And I've been debating on that with myself; I don't think my daddy and all those other men who went to war from Newport went because they couldn't see the Confederate side so much as they went because they belonged to a different generation—a different time.

That's how I see this other war shaping up." Caleb soberly considered Jerrie's solemn face. She was beginning to understand now.

"Not so much New Englanders against 'summer people' as the old versus the young. The staid folks against the disciples of change."

"But that'll be natural," Jerrie said, finally coming into the conversation. "You can't call that a war, Uncle Caleb."

The old man's shrewd puckered eyes sharpened. "Honey, there's all kinds of wars. You don't have to shoot at someone to scar a soul or make a lasting enemy. All you have to do is oppose their feelings. The 'summer people' are opposing local sentiment about the old church. It'll come to a head next summer, mark my word on it. It would have come to a head *this* summer, but the season's almost over now, so it's too late."

Caleb thought of something, threw back his head and laughed. The girl and boy waited. You had to know old Caleb's idiosyncrasies to understand him. Something had just occurred to him that was hilarious, but it would have some kind of social significance because few things Caleb did or thought lacked that kind of significance.

"Whatever happened to that furore a month back about the President visiting Newport?"

Again, Frank's blue gaze turned sharp as he studied the old man while Jerrie sat there puzzled by Caleb's seemingly pointless amusement.

Frank said, "Mister Adams; was that you?"

"Sure as night follows day, son, that was me."

"But why?"

"I wanted to see what they'd all do. You know, sometimes the best way in the world to shake up complacent folks is to hit them hard with something they dislike. So I simply started the tale circulating."

" There wasn't any truth in it?"

" None," replied Caleb, still near to chuckling. " None whatsoever. But it took folks' minds off the heat and poor lobster prices didn't it? Even the *Herald* came out with one of those predictably hidebound editorials."

Jerrie was beginning to scowl at old Uncle Caleb, but but she said nothing. Frank, on the other hand, tentatively smiled as he crossed his legs and loosely hung an arm over the back of the bench behind Jerrie.

" My father said the President would have to want to waste a lot of time to come to a place such as Newport where they'd never supported a Democratic President since the country was founded."

" He was right, son. What President would come here? The last one was Herbert Hoover and he was only passing through. And before that it was Cal Coolidge, but he didn't really reach Newport at all, but passed by us in a big ship."

Jerrie finally spoke. " Uncle Caleb, what will you do about this war you spoke of?"

" I? Jerrie I won't do a thing but sit and watch. You know what I've told you, child: The Lord didn't put me here to judge folks, only to laugh at them."

" And the church . . .?"

Caleb's faded, dancing eyes softened. A swift little grey shadow passed over his wrinkled features. " Your grandfather and great-grandfather are buried out back, Jerrie, the same as mine. The church is just an old building. Yes, I know; your folks were baptised there and married there. But it's no longer used, child, so they can make it over into anything anything respectable that is—but I'm just going to sit back and watch to see what they're going to do with all those old graves out back."

There was no mistaking the quieter tone the old man used now. He *did* have a personal interest after all; the other words were camouflage.

Frank shifted position; his shoulder brushed Jerric's shoulder. His arm still lay behind her on the old bench. " Mister Adams, graves are moved every day. There are lots of lovely places where they can re-locate those people."

The old man's gaze lingered on young Levinsky as he said, " Son; Newport keeps expanding. How many times can you move old stones and dust before they lose all their identity? Where do they move them next time, when the town expands out to wherever they'll put them this time?"

Frank didn't answer. He was thinking that for the first time since he'd known Caleb Adams, the old man had evidenced opposition to progress. Perhaps anyone would do that, though, when you scratched deeply enough beneath the surface and touched an unexpected nerve. Frank looked at his watch and stood up.

" I've got to get along." He looked at the girl. " Jerrie . . .?"

" You run along," she said, smiling at the tall, fair youth. " I want to hear more about this war, Frank."

" Well; will you go boating with me tomorrow?"

She nodded and her soft auburn hair danced. Frank smiled at them both, turned and struck out down the path to Caleb's rickety boat-landing. Jerrie turned a little to watch his departure and Caleb watched Jerrie without smiling at all. He had gloomy thoughts about those two. When she turned back Caleb asked if she'd like some cold lemonade. She declined and said, " You were telling us we were going to face difficult times, weren't you, Uncle Caleb?"

He nodded, fishing for an old pipe which he painstakingly loaded and fired up. " It's going to be awkward, Jerrie, but then you're a bright child. You could see there'd be trouble, couldn't you?"

" Well, yes," she murmured, watching smoke lift heavily in the hot, stillness. " But I thought it would be over—something else."

He seemed to know exactly what that ' something else ' was, for he said, " That's the oldest private fight on earth, Jerrie, and in some ways the hardest because, while the lovers usually triumph, then they have to prove for the rest of their lives they were right, while everyone else only has to sit around waiting for something to happen to prove they were wrong. Child; you can't afford any mistakes in your private war. Not one."

Jerrie looked at the distant river where Frank's boat cut a wide, clean swath as it swung wide, heading for his own elaborate dock. She didn't say anything and neither did Uncle Caleb. There wasn't really very much to say; *he* knew what she also knew, only he could be analytical about it because he was not emotionally involved. She couldn't be that way because she *was* emotionally involved. Very much so in fact, although neither her parents nor Frank's parents knew it yet.

CHAPTER FOUR

An Interlude at Home

FOR JERRIE the discontent was an elusive yet substantial sensation, something she'd experienced before but never for prolonged periods. Her normal nature was easy and pleasant. She'd never been a particularly self-conscious child even during the difficult transition era, from childhood to womanhood.

Going away to college had been the one big change of her entire life. But that wasn't unusual, it was the same with every child who made the same change. But it *was* different for Jerrie. For one thing, while most of her classmates and friends at college had come from big cities and were more sophisticated, Jerrie had constantly been surprised by the things she saw and heard. For another thing, because in Newport there were only her own kind of people, at college she saw brown and yellow and black people by the score, with the latter predominating, although it was noticeable too that the whiter were these black people, the better adjusted and intelligent they were.

College had been exciting, demanding, fulfilling; rather like living on the brink of a volcano because she'd never known when some wild demonstration might erupt or when some Great Man might appear to speak, or when some friend would pack up, white-faced, and wordlessly depart never to re-appear.

The appendicitis attack had ended all that for what she'd felt certain would be, at the most, a month, at the least a week or ten days.

The odd thing about the attack was that it didn't come suddenly as everyone assured her at the time was the rule. It came a little at a time, like cramps, and initially she didn't worry much about it. Then it became a listlessness, a feverish lassitude that lingered day after day with the fever steadily rising until she'd decided one week-end just to drive home.

The ensuing Monday she was in Newport's General Hospital with an ascetic-faced, gaunt man making an examination with a nurse and both her parents in attendance.

"Appendix," said the ascetic-faced man who was a physician and surgeon of considerable State-wide renown. "Nothing to worry about. This one happens to be very obliging. Usually they flare up overnight. This one for some reason is a slow starter. In any case, of course, it'll have to come out. I'll slate her for surgery this afternoon."

So the useless little blind-gut had come out and convalescence, while it had its bad first two days, was afterwards ordinary enough, right up until the day she sneezed and burst the stiches. Otherwise she'd have been back at college at the end of the month.

The scar was forming nicely, said the surgeon each time he saw Jerrie, and the last time, as her father and the doctor strode out on to the front porch, she heard her father mutter something in a quiet tone, and heard the physician say clearly, " Well, that's hardly in any way related to her operation, Mister Leavitt, and I could only guess about it anyway because I'm not learned in that field. There are some good men down in the city if you'd care to take her there. I'll send you some names."

She'd heard her father mutter again in that low tone, then he'd returned to the house alone, smiling and wanting to know if she'd like a dish of ice-cream.

She could guess what her father had said to the physician and it made her blush. Both parents had sensed the change in her, the new moodiness, the long periods of total silence. It was as though she had a secret, and of course she did have, although several times over the past week or so she'd wanted to blurt it out and let them make the most of it. She knew, of course how they felt about the ' summer people ' and although she also knew her parents were a lot less vitriolic than most of the other natives, she also knew they would be stunned if she told them she'd been seeing Frank Levinsky.

It had started out innocently enough, but then most things do. They'd met the summer before. Actually, she'd met Meyer first and hadn't liked him for the same reason most of the natives didn't; he was too loud, too assertive, too confident. But she'd also been able to understand Meyer. It hadn't been any of those Freudian things people said at all; Meyer'd never felt insecure or unwanted or rejected in his life. He was loud because he had a zest for life. He was confident because most of the time he'd been right, and his brashness came from pure environment. He'd told her once when he'd taken her boating that this was the one thing he'd had no experience with

B

and feared—water. But even then he'd proved a quick learner and a careful mariner. He'd then explained how it had been with him down in New York City where if a boy didn't learn to fight early, think fast, move swiftly, he got lost in the backwash. He'd also said at that time that his brother Frank had never really belonged in the city. Frank was too quiet, too thoughtful. He was somewhere in the borderland between being a romanticist and a dreamer.

" The kind of guy who writes books," Meyer had said. " Nice enough, you know. Too nice perhaps. Anyway, Frank belongs in a place like Newport. He's got so damned little commercial instinct. Mother wanted Frank to be an attorney. My dad used to tell her: ' My God, Madge, you'd have the only kid in the world who'd bleed for both clients. Frank isn't an instinctive killer; he'd make a lousy lawyer.' "

Jerrie had been piqued, so Meyer arranged it and after that Frank, who *was* a sailor, took her boating while Meyer, standing back and watching this phenomenon— his quiet brother beating Meyer's time with a girl— smiled a little ruefully because he'd just lost the prettiest girl in Newport.

But Meyer neither moped nor turned reproachful. He and his brothers were very different, true, but they were still brothers. Furthermore, Meyer was never really serious with girls despite what he told them. He revealed as much one time when the three of them were fishing at the mouth of the Kanaki, where it mingled with the salt seawater.

" A man's got lots of time. That talk of marrying young so's you can grow up with your kids is a lot of bunk. You couldn't grow up with your kids if you wanted to because they wouldn't let you. It's better to make something of yourself first. Know what I mean? Get something; a business, a career, something that'll help make a marriage last."

Frank had laughed and Jerrie had smiled. It all made Meyer seem so old and worldly.

But that had been the summer Jerrie'd turned eighteen with a new life just beyond her personal horizon. Now she was nineteen and had grown very fond of Frank. Too fond, actually. It would have been so much easier if she'd never neglected telling her parents, but she had and because she was honest with herself she knew exactly *why* she had.

Not particularly because he was Jewish although that certainly figured in it. Nor because he belonged to the ' summer people ' clique, although that too entered into it. But primarily because she knew—had heard—things her parents said about the Levinskys. True things, which didn't make it any easier for Jerrie. Meyer Senior was shrewd and crude and ungrammatical and flamboyant. He was needlessly profligate with his money, of which he had an inordinate amount, both in the way he spent it in town, and also the way he threw it away on his estate along the river.

It had always deeply wounded the New England soul to see anyone show disrespect for money. To paint a boat-dock was unheard of. To plant an acre of lawn that sloped from house to the river was sheer folly, as was buying a tractor-lawnmower and hiring a man to run the thing all summer-long just to have the immense lawn always properly manicured.

Having three powerful and expensive boats instead of

the usual one economy model soured the natives towards the Levinskys, and of course this latest gambit—trying to turn their abandoned, ramshackle but properly aged and historic old Episcopalian church into a roadhouse or whatever he called it, sealed their disapproval.

Jerrie came home from college in mid-term for her appendectomy and was immediately immersed in this latest outrage. She and Frank discussed it. He stated his father's view very calmly, then turned right around and sympathised with the native viewpoint. She told him, one day as they sat in the shade of a giant oak not far from the river where they'd come to picnic, that he'd have to take one side or the other, and he'd looked at her in surprise.

" Why? I'm neither a native nor an ingenue, Jerrie. It won't make one bit of difference to me whether Newport has a church or discothéque."

" It's more than that, Frank. It's like Uncle Caleb said —it's going to be a rallying factor for the clans."

" All right; I'm willing to concede that, Jerrie, but why do I have to rally to *either* side?"

She'd felt annoyed with him for just a second, then smiled as she said, " What are you, Frank, a ' summer-person ' or a native?"

" I'm neither, Jerrie. I'm me. Frank Levinsky. I don't come up here every summer to tear down churches *or* to build discothéques. I come here because I love it. Someday I'm going to live here all year round. Maybe buy a business or something. Maybe—get married here. Anyway, just because I'm here doesn't mean I have to always take sides, does it?"

She squirmed and had her first misgivings about Frank

Levinsky. Maybe, as she'd heard people say of all ' summer people ', he *was* different. But in any case, when he said he wanted to settle permanently in Newport and in the same breath admitted he also wished to remain personally detached, uninvolved, it just didn't make sense to her.

But they didn't argue. They never actually argued. Frank was a hard person to get angry or impassioned. Even when he'd knocked Jonah Sutherland unconscious in Rosie's Café he hadn't been angry. In a way, too, she complemented him because her own temper wasn't explosive nor fiery; it was slow-kindling, hot-burning, but compounded more of gradual indignation than of unreasoning passion.

She didn't see Frank for the first two weeks after the operation. But the next two weeks she saw him often. They talked of college too; he had more odd ideas about that. One of them was that college created more educated damned fools than anything else. He'd steadfastly declined to return after his second year. Another idea, hardly original and not irrefutable either, was that girls went to college less to become professionals in the competitive world than to catch husbands, but even if they failed in this all-important function of the co-educational system, they rarely ended up as anything likely to excel, unless of course being a schoolteacher was a subliminal achievement.

The last time they were together they went fishing on the far side of the mile-wide river, and ended up exploring a swampy tangle of deserted tidelands beyond which stood a large, gaunt and forlorn old house upon a low, oak-studded grass hill.

Obviously at one time there had been a thrifty farm beyond the old house, and just as obviously people of substance had lived there. Now though, only bats and racoons and wood rats lived in the house while deer and other wild animals roamed the clear fields.

Frank made the proper guess when he said, " It's on the wrong side of the river. You can see Newport from here easy enough, but to get there by land you'd have to drive backroads for fifty miles."

She said she'd ask Uncle Caleb sometime who'd lived in the house and tilled the acreage, then they returned to the boat with a setting sun burnishing the sky a coppery hue, and set out for home.

She was due to return to college the next day so neither of them was very talkative on the ride back. The summer season would end soon. The Levinskys would return to the city. An entire winter would pass, and a blustery springtime as well, before they'd see each other again.

He held her hand as they parted at the wharf below the town and said he had a lot of sorting out to do this coming winter, but that by next summer he'd probably have answers to a lot of things that he'd let slide during the gorgeous summer.

He hadn't offered to kiss her and she too had hung back from that. But she was very fond of him. Still, the odd things he said at times kept her clear of any deep entanglement.

After they parted she walked home in the gloaming with troubled thoughts. When she saw the lights in the parlour and dining-room she wondered if she'd been wise keeping her private life so totally private. Then she procrastinated. She told herself she had all winter to do some sorting-out of her own feelings and thoughts, so she wouldn't say anything now.

But, for some odd reason, she no longer was so eager to get back to the hectic campus life. From the porch she turned and looked beyond the town to the sea, following up the beaches to where the river spilled its salt-free blood into the greeny sea. But his boat was out of sight.

CHAPTER FIVE

A Conflict of Interests

JOHN LEAVITT'S two companions in the Selectmen's chambers were a banker and a successful plumber. When the Levinsky application came up the banker said. " Stall it."

He wouldn't have said that if there'd been an audience in the chambers but, although all meetings were open to the public, people rarely ever came to watch. Unless, of course, there was something important on the agenda. The old church was important, but still no one showed up, either because they were too busy, too tired, or too certain what would happen to Levinsky's application to purchase the old property.

The plumber agreed with the banker. " Stall it, John. Season's just about over anyway. 'Nother couple of weeks and they'll start closing up the cottages and heading back to the city."

John shrugged. He didn't object to stalling it, but that didn't really solve anything. Levinsky would be back the following summer and, if John had read him right that morning in the store, Levinsky would want a concise explanation. He'd recognise procrastination as quickly as anyone else would. John said, " Let's discuss it. There's nothing else on the agenda anyway, unless it's the increase in pay the police want, and we can't give that until we've found another source of revenue, so let's talk about this Levinsky matter."

The plumber was willing but the banker fastened a cold, analytical look upon John and said, " Wouldn't be anything personal in it, would there, John?"

For a second Jerrie's father looked blank, then he smiled. " I've talked to the man once—in the store last month."

The banker and plumber exchanged a look. The banker said no more for a while but fell to doodling with his pencil on the lined yellow tablet in front of him. In front of each of them in fact.

The plumber was careful when he said, " I just don't see the reason, John. Why does Newport need a disco-thèque? The young people have plenty of places to go. In my opinion Levinsky would be making a bad invest-ment. Granting he's got the money, it's still not a sound investment in my eyes."

John's reply was casual. " You don't have to worry about that, Ed. It's his money; if he wants to throw it around we can't prevent it. The only thing that ought to concern us is whether selling him the old church is in the best interests of the town."

"Damn it, no," growled the banker, a bulldog-type older man. "It's *not* in the best interests of the town. How can it be? Newport neither needs or ought to have one of those Frenchified coffee houses. Last summer when the missus and I visited California you wouldn't believe the type of people we saw in those—discothéques. Dirty, unshaven, irresponsible, worthless. When I first heard the talk about what Levinsky intended I felt like going out there and reading him off.

"I say the best interests of Newport will be served by keeping something like this from happening here. I say stall Levinsky until he forgets his crazy idea."

John came right back. "Charley; stalling isn't going to be enough. I talked for a half-hour with Levinsky at the store last month. He's not a fool."

"I didn't say he was."

"Then let's make the decision to turn him down out in the open and let him at least see we're not mealy in this thing."

The banker looked up at John. "You don't really care?"

"Why should I?"

"Well; I don't know. But I've heard Frank Levinsky will operate the coffee house and . . . get some local girl to help him."

John began to have a bad feeling in the pit of his stomach. Both the other men were watching him so he kept his face and eyes totally blank. "You mean Jerrie?" he asked.

B*

The banker spread his hands. " Well; they're always together, John. What else should people think?"

Always together! It hit John hard. So hard in fact he had to fight to keep his expression from showing the low blow he'd just absorbed. He said, speaking quietly and slowly, " Charley, we're probing far afield. Our concern is whether or not we should let Levinsky have the building. Beyond that—"

" Beyond that," interrupted the plumber, " we've got the duty to try and anticipate things, John. It's *not* just selling him the old church. It's what he means to do with it, and how *that* will affect the town. I'm with Charley on it; stall him. Let him think about it all winter and maybe by next tourist-season he'll have forgot the whole darned thing."

The door opened and closed. They all looked round. Caleb was stalking a chair beyond the railed-off area where the Selectmen sat. He was clean-shaven and freshly dressed, in itself some kind of warning signal, but he merely nodded as he gingerly eased down upon the chair, and smiled.

He was the only spectator although there were ranks of empty chairs capable of accommodating at least two hundred viewers or protesters, whichever they happened to have to hold, now and then.

John said, " Caleb, did you want something in particular?"

The old man fingered the brim of his hat in his lap. " Just wondering what you men had decided on the old church was all."

The banker and plumber turned quiet, curious gazes upon Caleb, neither of them speaking though, perhaps unwilling to open up something they might have difficulty in closing.

John said, " We were just discussing it," and turned to face his companions. They each slid him a look and fell to contemplating the pads in front of each place at the large old table. What they'd just been saying hadn't been at all what they'd have said had spectators been beyond the railing, which was now the case.

The banker cleared his throat. " John I don't see that we can give any decision on Mister Levinsky's application to purchase the old church until all of us have made a thorough study of his offer."

The plumber took this same tack. " I'd like time on this. I've been so busy lately I haven't had a chance to look into the matter."

John nodded. Under the circumstances he knew where the other Selectmen stood anyway. He started to write something on his pad—a note amending the Minutes to show the Levinsky application had been temporarily shelved pending a further investigation of all factors. Then old Caleb interrupted.

" Gentlemen; the church is useless. You can't even get the State to take it over as an official historical landmark; there are fifty churches just as old within two hundred miles, and most of 'em at one time or another had George Washington or someone in the pews. Our church just hasn't ever been outstanding."

The banker looked coldly at old Adams. " You're suggesting the community dispose of it, Mister Adams?"

Caleb vigorously nodded. " Yes. It's in pretty poor shape right now, Charley, and if all these incensed folks who revere it so cussed much weren't plain hypocrites, why haven't they gone down there and painted it, fixed the busted windows, chopped weeds out front, and made it look less like an eyesore?"

The banker declined to answer but the plumber said, "Mister Adams; do you know what a discothéque is?"

"Coffee house," snapped old Caleb, who hadn't known two weeks earlier but knew now because Frank Levinsky had partially explained it to him.

The plumber was rebuked and fell silent. But John Leavitt, who'd known Caleb Adams all his life, turned to study the old man, then say, "What's in your mind, Uncle Cal?"

Caleb was prepared for that question too. "The graves," he fired right back. "Not the building, boys; it's just wood and nails and flaking white paint. But what happens to the graves out back? My parents and grandparents are buried there. So are your folks, Ed, and John you were on the clean-up committee for six years and helped keep weeds off the plot your folks have. What I want to know, gentlemen, is what you propose doing with my parents and the others?"

Charley and Ed exchanged a look. The banker seemed enormously relieved about something. He said, "John; there's your answer to the whole problem. We just can't allow the old church to be turned into a coffee house by Meyer Levinsky. That's hallowed ground out there."

John's slow anger began simmering. Charley had said all that in the most triumphant tone he could have employed, but it wasn't an honest statement; neither Charley nor Ed had given those old graves a single thought until Caleb had brought them up. Now, they were using the graves as a pious buttress to their personal disapproval of the entire Levinsky project, which, of course—although both would have fiercely denied it—was based on personal animosity towards ' summer people ' in general and brash, loud Meyer Levinsky in particular.

But John had something else troubling him so was unable to give his full attention to this matter. Not, as he morbidly told himself, that it mattered one damned bit, they would out-vote him if he asked for a decision, so he leaned back in his chair and said, " I'll agree to a delay while we consider the entire affair from every standpoint."

Charley smiled broadly. He boldly winked across at the plumber who loosened in his chair looking satisfied. There was then a brief discussion concerning the police department's request for additional pay. That was disposed of very simply: There just was not an extra, uncommitted, red cent in the town treasury, so, sympathetic as the Selectmen were to the formal request, they just could not do a thing about it.

That ended the meeting. It was shortly after ten o'clock, and this was gratifying because, aside from receiving no reimbursement for acting as elected officials of the town, the job at times became very irksome and made its people lose a lot of sleep.

As the banker and plumber left, side by side and patently pleased with what had come to pass, old Caleb waited by the door for John Leavitt, patiently standing there until John had finished his rough draft of the Minutes, which he'd taken home and which Georgia would type up for inclusion in one of the dusty old books of Minutes lining one wall of the Selectmen's rooms.

As John finally reached for his hat, went over to turn out the lights, Caleb said, " What happened before I got up here, John?"

He eased the old man out, closed and locked the doors then said, " Nothing, Uncle Cal. Just talk."

" About the church?"

" Yes. And—something else. But that didn't have anything to do with local affairs."

They went warily down the dark stairway and out into the soft summer night. There was a faint hint of cold-to-come in the scent and feel of the weather. Caleb stood a moment to sniff and look skyward, then, when John offered to drive Caleb down to the river, the old man accepted with alacrity. He owned no automobile; unless he could hitch a ride he had a long walk from his place to town. Newport had no public transportation and the man who owned the town's two mongrel taxi-cabs charged what to Caleb Adams was a piratical rate just to come fetch him, then haul him back home again.

As they scooted round and headed down along the dark commercial part of the town Caleb said, " John; if they move the graves, where can they put them that they won't have to move them again in five years? You got to understand the reason I'm interested. Within that many years I'll be under that same sod."

John looked over and back again. He didn't offer any of those platitudes most people would have to that statement; he was a New Englander, which meant he was an honest man. Old Caleb was probably very right. To a man of seventy or better, five years was a very long time.

" I don't know," he murmured. Then, because the

graves weren't really what was etched most sharply into his consciousness, he said, "Cal; tell me something: Have you seen Jerrie with Frank Levinsky very often?"

The old man didn't answer for so long a time that John turned. Then Caleb said, "They come over and sit with me now and then, John. Or go boating. Fishing and picnicking."

"Often?"

Caleb couldn't say. Or *wouldn't* say. "What's wrong with that, John? She's nigh twenty. He's nigh twenty-three or more."

"Well, Cal, everyone seems to know about it but her mother and me. It's like she's ashamed of it."

Caleb snorted. "Not that child, John. She's not the kind to do things she'd be ashamed of. But if you thought they were extra good friends would you have encouraged it? I don't think so. Maybe it was just easier to have peace than it was to tell her folks everything." They were at the river and old Caleb got out of the car, leaned down and said, "Thank you, John. Thank you very much. Tell Georgia I asked after her. Good night."

"Good night."

John turned slowly and drove home slowly. He'd forgotten about the old church entirely.

CHAPTER SIX

The Winter Moon

MADGE'S REACTION to what John told her was slow. Jerrie had been back at college over a week now, Madge had her own civic interests and besides, as she told John over breakfast, if two youngsters saw each other more than twice in Newport it became an example of classic undying love.

John didn't push it; in the cool light of morning it did begin to appear that his own reaction had been severe. Moreover it was very pleasant just to switch to something else. Madge asked about the old church. He told her it would remain as it was for at least the balance of the year. He didn't bother explaining that he'd pushed the other Selectmen for a decision on the Levinsky application-to-purchase in order to get the problem settled one way or the other, because in the clear sparkling early morning over coffee and cereal with his wife, that didn't seem very important either.

Something the banker had said became noticeably correct as time passed; the summer season was over. If this might have stirred sadness in anyone it had to be the ' summer people ' because native New Englanders looked forward just as much to their grey-white winters as to their summers. Perhaps sometimes even more so, for when the roads became almost impassable with snow, they had only the most hardy outlanders to contend with on the ski slopes and frozen ponds.

The people left, a few each day, until near the middle of September they were almost all gone, their cottages or estates closed and padlocked, their boat-landings forlornly empty, their lawn furniture securely stowed away. or, as Caleb had once said, " It's like they struck their colours when they haul in their lawn furniture."

Meyer Levinsky stopped by the emporium the day before he herded his tribe southward. The moment John Leavitt saw him enter he could have plotted what would ensue between them with pinpoint accuracy because by law the minutes of each meeting of the Town Fathers was published in the newspaper.

Levinsky was affable and quiet as he greeted John, but he was also straight to the point. " I see in the paper I didn't come out so good with the Selectmen, Mister Leavitt."

" They wanted more time, Mister Levinsky."

" Sure." Levinsky's blue eyes were steady as stones. " Mister Leavitt, I'll live if I don't make the discothéque. I'll probably have one less migraine headache even. But if I don't do it, believe me, someone else will. Maybe not with the old church, but somewhere around town, and if you're real lucky they may run a decent place, if not it'll be a typical discothéque, dirty physically and mentally and spiritually. And you'll have deserved it, Mister Leavitt."

After Levinsky left, Emil Franzen came in and said,

" I just saw Levinsky leaving. Did he read in the paper where the Selectmen cut him down?"

" He saw where we shelved his application until we can make a proper study," said John, hewing to the line of what actually happened.

Emil's voice was sly as he said, " That's the only way to handle 'em John," then the wealthy old farmer strode along deeper into the store to make a purchase.

John forgot Meyer Levinsky as the morning moved along. In the afternoon it got very hot, not unusually hot for late summer, which actually was the hottest time of the year, but hot enough to drive people indoors, and of course that was reflected in the slack afternoon trade.

Junior Walton, the town drunk, seemed to suffer less than most folks for some reason, and he was stone-sober which was worthy of note in itself as he entered the emporium for liquorice root and a dime's worth of asafoetida. It was reasonable to assume he meant to chew the liquorice root, and it was probable he meant to put the asafoetida into a Bull Durham sack and toss it into the pond out back of his shack where mosquitoes bred in frenetic abandon. Asofoetida was supposed to make the water unfit for larvae but as far as actual tests on that score, there probably never had been any. But if paw and grandpaw tossed a Bull Durham sack of asafoetida into a pond or trough to prevent larvae from hatching, there would be many sons and grandsons who'd do the same without ever bothering to ascertain the benefits, if any.

Madge came by, drooping, and John took her into the gloomy old office whose sole redeeming social element was that during heatwaves it was blessedly cool. He got her a bottle of soda-pop, turned up the old noiseless overhead ceiling-fan and smiled at her wan look. Madge had never been able to live with very much heat. She took the fierce New England winters in fine shape, but heat melted her physically and mentally.

She told him they'd had a letter from Jerrie. She was working frantically to make up lost time. Jerrie felt certain she'd be able to catch up. She wanted to know how things were going at home. She asked about the old church but did not once mention the Levinskys, which was a minor relief to her father although by now he'd almost got over his feelings of some time back. Jerrie said she was looking forward to the Thanksgiving Day celebration and the week-long vacation.

Aside from that Madge knew very little. The Levinskys had departed; had packed their three cars and headed down to the city again. Very few of the ' summer people ' were still extant. A few of the men were talking of returning for hunting season but that happened every year and they didn't return. Obviously, a warm apartment in the city did a lot towards ameliorating the already atrophying hunting instincts which invariably included some definite discomforts.

After Madge left, Caleb showed up at the store, red in the face from his long walk, and panting for a bottle of soda-pop, which he drank leaning upon the deserted counter and telling John that Meyer Levinsky had hired him at fifty dollars a month to keep an eye on the Levinsky place. But, actually, there were very few burglaries, and that was unusual in a place where perhaps one-half the residences sat empty for half of each year. But, of course, since tourism had become one of Newport's economic mainstays, the police department was touchy on the subject of inadequate police protection for the empty homes and made vigilant patrols almost every day.

Caleb asked about Jerrie. John told him what Madge'd recalled from their daughter's last letter. Caleb sipped soda and nodded with a far-away look in his eyes. After a while he said, " John; you were upset that night they took up Mister Levinsky's application." He looked at Leavitt with a rheumy, shrewd pair of old eyes. " Now you're not, eh?"

John, disliking the topic, said shortly, " No " and would have changed the subject but Caleb spoke first.

" Well now; the forewarned are the fore-armed. You've got all winter to figure things out, which is plenty of time to work your way through just about every kind of problem that might arise next summer. You know, not every father gets a nice winter-long respite like that. Of course the thing to do is make up your mind about your own feelings first. That way, if you're wise at all, you won't come off next summer smellin' like a skunk."

Caleb's repeated reference to ' next summer ' made John consider the old man dourly. " You talk like next summer is going to be some kind of ultimatum, Caleb."

" It is, son, it is," agreed the old man, finishing his bottle of soda-pop, placing it on the counter and straightening up. " Levinsky will be back and *he'll* have had all winter to do his thinkin' too. And Jerrie'll be back. Caleb didn't elaborate on that, he simply smiled, nodded, and went over where the clerks were standing, gossiping. He had a couple of small purchases to make.

John went to the office for his hat and light coat. He wouldn't be needed any more today at the store if the present trend was any indication of the amount of trade they'd do. He went home, had a cold glass of lemonade out back under the big tree with Madge and did not mention his talk with Caleb Adams.

The heatwave passed, the leaves crisped around their edges, wild colour came to mountainsides and the nights turned cool. The people engaged in the maple syrup industry set out their pots and tools, greased their sleds and otherwise prepared for the season ahead. Woodcutters came from door to door to peddle their summer-cured offering, and even the people who had oil heaters in their basements still bought a few cord. A New England night was long and dark and icily cold; it wouldn't have seemed right at all not to have a crackling fire in stove or fireplace, despite the oil heater.

The first rind of frost appeared on the fourteenth of September, which was about normal for the area, and after that the leaves went really wild. There were crimson, yellow, orange, white, even blue and black leaves floating down from trees in yards or on the farms or farther back, where the wilderness areas ran for rocky, hilly miles.

The two sweetest scents on earth—hot coffee and wood-smoke—presaged real winter, which wouldn't actually arrive for another month or two. Autumn was a hazy time of year. Apples turned scarlet, schoolchildren trooped to classrooms, every step crunched over crackly leaves, the air took on a metallic fragrance peculiar to this one season, animals turned fluffy and people dug out their woollen skirts and shirts, their long-legged unmentionables, showed sparkling eyes and rosy cheeks.

If the heat lasted into autumn to obscure further the

blue-blazing distances it was called Indian Summer. But this year the heat departed by the end of August, the cold arrived immediately thereafter, and although the peculiar smoke-haze lingered, autumn and winter were hand in hand.

The snow came early too. It usually arrived right after Thanksgiving; between Thanksgiving and Christmas. This year it came in mid-October, just a light skiff the first time but the cold would not depart again until the following spring so it might just as well have snowed hard.

Jerrie came home pink and bright and full of youthful effervescence for the holidays. She'd made up all but one of her classes—maths—and she cheerfully admitted she'd never be able to replace Emily Trotten as book-keeper at the store anyway, nor did she expect to become a learned physicist, so it didn't really matter. Her father might have argued the point but in the face of her sturdy beauty and abundant health his resolve evaporated like smoke.

Thanksgiving was a New England holiday. All the rest of the nation also observed it, but in New England it had a special significance. Originally designed to show appreciation for good harvests, it still to a considerable degree meant the same thing only now it was celebrated by more wage-earners in factories and shopkeepers than countrymen.

And of course after Thanksgiving came Christmas, close enough so that for several weeks the goodwill and brotherhood remained strong in everyone's spirit and attitude.

This period in Newport was the best time of year for natives. All the heat-abrasions of summer were missing.

There were few strangers in town, no ' summer people ', no noisy speedboats on the river, nothing to remind anyone of what they'd had to put up with only a month or two back.

Caleb came to dinner on Thanksgiving at the Leavitt place, along with three or four other relatives, there was mulled ale and wine, and also honest New England applejack, soft as a mother's love with the kick of an army mule.

Traditionally, the head of the household—John—carved the forty-pound golden-brown aromatic turkey. It was a good time, and if people tended to blur all Thanksgiving celebrations together, that only aided in making each one a commemoration to the basic convictions of the people.

Jerrie kissed Uncle Caleb under the mistletoe to everyone's delight, and the old man's rheumy eyes, more sunken this year than before, showed a surge of masculine appreciation. When they were off to one side he asked if she'd been getting letters from the city. He didn't mention any names. She responded with a smile and a slow wink.

" Once a week."

" Pshaw; when I was young I'd write one every two days."

Her eyes danced at him. " Postage stamps were only one cent in those days, Uncle Caleb. Now they cost five cents."

That was true enough. " And what's he doing?"

" Writing a book."

Caleb blinked. " A book? I didn't know . . . but yes, that'd be right for Frank, wouldn't it?"

She nodded, sharing with old Caleb a special know-

came over flush-faced from the kitchen and smiled on them both. "You act like a pair of conspirators," she said. "Uncle Caleb, if you want to wash up we'll be eating in about ten minutes." After Caleb had dutifully marched off, Madge looked at her daughter. She'd always been able to see where Jerrie resembled her, and also where she looked most like John. She was a strikingly handsome girl. Madge sighed, for no particular reason, and kissed Jerrie on the cheek. Then she had to hasten back to the kitchen.

CHAPTER SEVEN

Burning of the Church

CHRISTMAS CAME and went. New Year's Eve finished the winter time revelry for the older people but it only set a snowy stage for the younger ones. Jerrie managed to twist an ankle on the ski slopes before she had to go back to school. It didn't hinder her driving back but, as she reported by letter, it slowed her a bit on racing from class to class at college.

At the store, popular demand changed entirely from

what it had been several months before, and anachronistic or not John arranged for the delivery of three cord of pine and fir for the huge old pot-bellied stove where people stood and gossiped, backs to the considerable heat, faces towards the front window where the snowfall always looked best.

In his father's and grandfather's day that ugly iron behemoth had been the rallying point for Newport in wintertime. It was there such topics as politics, national or local, were threshed out, rarely to everyone's satisfaction but threshed out nonetheless. Also, around that stove, were made decisions which had affected the life of Newport for a hundred years. Of course John'd had an oil-burner installed in the cellar with discreet vents along the base-shoe all over the big old building, but people still stood around the stove.

Madge once said that if John disposed of the old iron stove he'd lose half his customers. True or not, the stove stayed, and not entirely as a symbol either, for Caleb among others had repeatedly stated as fact that no heat ever devised could even approximate the penetrating variety of heat that came from an honest, wood-burning, iron stove, and John secretly agreed.

During the winter, except for storekeepers and those engaged in bleeding maple trees, there wasn't very much actual labour indulged in. Moreover, the days were too short, the ground frozen to a depth of eighteen inches, and no one had much inclination in that direction anyway.

In January they got a snowfall that closed the roads for two days, which was not unusual, so local life became more sedentary than ever. John would have let one of the clerks go except that he'd have been so hard to replace in March when things picked up again.

Otherwise, Newport drank coffee, gossiped, visited round among the neighbours, went ice-skating, ski-ing, hunting, to the Parents-Teachers Associations meetings at the school, and marked time until spring arrived again.

There was no sense of urgency about anything during wintertime. Newport became and remained a closed-off world inhabited exclusively by descendants of its Puritan founders. Its amusements were simple; the movie-house showed Westerns and situation-comedies. The Italian pictures were safely stored in round cans.

In February the only ripple occurred when Caleb caught a ride in from the river with Emil Franzen to tell Miss Trotten—John was out shopping with Madge over in Beaver Falls, the county seat—that Frank Levinsky was living at the Levinsky place.

Miss Trotten sniffed. " In the dead of winter? Don't tell me we're to be invaded by them in wintertime too?"

Caleb chuckled. He'd known Emily Trotten a very long while. In fact, although there'd been a barrier of a quarter of a century between them at the time, he'd once taken to sending her flowers. But that hadn't come to anything and now old Caleb wasn't so sure the Good Lord hadn't properly intervened, because Emily had turned more sour as the years had passed.

" He's writing a book, Emily. I met him out gathering wood yesterday in a foot of snow. He said he wanted to be absolutely alone to concentrate."

Emily sniffed again. " I don't think he'll have any trouble on that score, Caleb. Folks'll leave him alone all right."

Caleb had gone back with Franzen by the time John returned to the store to hear from Miss Trotten that Frank Levinsky was down at the river estate of his parents. John's reaction was difficult to classify; Jerrie woudn't be home again until the spring vacation, but the distance wasn't so far she couldn't drive back and forth very easily—if she knew. Of course if she didn't know . . .

" What did Caleb say he was doing down there?"

" Writing a book. He wants privacy to concentrate. I imagine he'll get his privacy all right. At least as far as *I'm* concerned he will!"

John took that home to Madge. And of course it was common knowledge by the following day anyway, as most things were in wintertime Newport when folks had more leisure to look into the affairs of friends and neighbours. But it caused only a minor ripple. The fact that Frank didn't appear in town helped things too, plus events in other parts of the world which were more uneasily assimilated for evening newscasts. The United States involvement in faraway places sent many a Newportian secretly to his encyclopaedia in order that the following day he—or she—would be able to discourse more knowledgeably about places they'd never even heard of until the night before.

Then Frank drove to the emporium for coal-oil. All winter long the people of New England suffered in patient silence when weighty snow snapped electric lines. Kerosene lamps then were pressed into use. Frank also had other purchases to make. He looked good in an expensive checked pure wool shirt, heavy trousers and lace-boots. Even his coat—call a Mackinaw after the place where it had been manufactured—was proper winter attire.

He was polite but minimal in conversation. The men standing around the pot-bellied stove watched his every move with their eyes but had no comment to offer. Not until he left anyway.

John waited on him. He bought no fancy things and his hands showed callouses from chopping wood. When he bought two red wedges and a sledgehammer—for frozen wood—John wondered if he'd ever used either before.

They put the purchases in the small foreign car out front, nearly hidden by snow that lined the kerbings, and John stood in the late-day chill watching the little automobile gingerly head down towards the river over the ice-glazed roads.

He told Madge about that too, when they were having their last cup of coffee for the day in front of a blazing fireplace that evening. She'd showed slight interest which, of course, meant she'd never really put any stock in those summertime rumours.

In February the police provided a source of discussion by discovering that the abandoned Episcopal church was being used by a party of four tramps as a residence.

People living within the immediate vicinity had seen lights there at night, and one particularly cold day smoke was seen rising from the fireplace stack.

The tramps were typical dissolutes; neither young nor old, worthless, whining men, four in number who said they'd been heading for Montreal in Canada but hadn't been able to hitch a ride out of Newport since the last blizzard so had taken up residence in what was patently an abandoned old building.

The police chief gave them warmer accommodations until something could be devised for getting them on their way. One of the men was surly and darkly resentful. He made no threats but he made a promise. He told his turnkey he'd remember Newport for jailing him without just cause. He'd remember the fat merchants and sleek farmers.

Three days later when the chief of police arranged for the men to continue northward in a National Guard truck which was going as far as the border, he released the four men, stood them to a meal at Rosie's, then forgot about them.

The following day the old church burnt to the ground.

The fire was evidently started sometime in the night. It wasn't noted until about three in the morning when some light sleeper in the area smelled smoke, looked out, then ran to the telephone to have the operator summon the Newport Volunteer Fire Brigade.

But it burned too swiftly even with a cake-icing layer of snow on the roof. The wood was old, tinder-dry, very combustible. About all that could be saved was the bell, and it wouldn't burn although when the steeple collapsed the bell had been badly cracked in its tumble to the frozen earth. By daybreak nothing was left. Ashes smouldered and hissed, the outline of the structure was etched in square black lines against the muddy earth where heat had melted away snow in all directions for almost two hundred feet. John, a member of the fire brigade, helped re-coil and load the hoses with hands so cold the fingers worked only with painful effort. The banker was there, helping. He said, " There goes the discothéque," and got no answer from John nor seemed to expect one.

The day turned bright with a cold but brilliant sun shining. Every few minutes the sound of snow falling by

To Face the Sun

the ton off roofs or sheds made a constant dull sound. At the emporium the natural subject under discussion was the fire, but not until the chief of police came in to exhibit a melted bottle, charred gauze or some other rough cloth wired round the bottle, and an assortment of what he claimed were matches and wicks, did anyone actually consider arson as the cause of the blaze.

But as the chief explained it sonorously and methodically, making a mock-up atop the counter, the bottle had held kerosene; the rags, tied round the bottle and held by the wire, had been saturated, and that snake-like, very frail ash on the paper, had been a long wick. The thing had been ignited by the matches through an ingenious device which employed a tiny lighted wax candle which burned slowly, thus did not touch off the little bundle of matches until perhaps three or four hours after the candle had been lit, and after that it was all very obvious. The matches had lit the wick, the wick had burnt to the bottle, which had ignited both outside and inside, and the church had then been destroyed from the resulting fire at an hour when it would be very unlikely anyone would be around to see it and stop it.

" So," said the police chief to John and the others, " I've telephoned Montreal giving the descriptions and names of those tramps—of one tramp in particular—so that we can extradite the man or men, and charge them with arson, which is a felony."

The church actually was no loss. It had been repeatedly claimed the old building was a fire-threat to all the nearby buildings, and now there was an agreement that had this fire occurred during tinder-dry summertime, it most probably would have engulfed several residences.

Whether nostalgic old-timers were saddened or not, the church was gone. That it had only about six months earlier been the subject of much debate seemed rather pointless now. As the banker had said, " There went the discothéque."

John was of two minds on the matter. He was sorry that the church was gone. He was also relieved that it was gone. If Meyer Levinsky returned next summer still with his wish to make a coffee house, now he'd have to seek another location, and whatever people thought of a discothéque in Newport, at least there would not, next time, be the emotionalism involved, because there were no other vacant churches around.

Madge wrote of the disaster to Jerrie and received word back that Jerrie thought the arsonist had done Newport a favour. Jerrie didn't elaborate, so her parents didn't know whether she meant the arsonist had done away with a fire-trap, or whether she meant he'd done away with a source of friction.

The arsonist was never returned to Newport. The Canadians arrested the man on a narcotics charge and got him convicted. He admitted firing the old church between the time the chief of police bought him a decent dinner at Rosie's and the time the National Guard truck hauled him away. He was, obviously, a very accomplished arsonist to have had everything ready at such short notice.

In March, during a thaw, the Selectmen took bids on cleaning up the mess. By the end of March only a dark stain and some crumbling mortar footings showed where the old church had stood. Behind it, gravestones which hadn't been visible to the roadway as long as the old church stood, were now plainly in sight. Someone mentioned planting a boxwood hedge out front to hide the headstones. Someone else said the town ought to turn the entire area into a cemetery, landscape it and let it stand as a reminder that Newport was an old town.

John's objection to this was elemental. In the first place there would be a graveyard right in the centre of the city, which didn't seem proper. In the second place the plot of ground was hardly large enough to accommodate more than another hundred or so graves. And in the third place the cost of maintenance would be exorbitant.

Nothing was decided because there was no urgency, and meanwhile April came in with a bursting of buds and a thawing of earth, with gusty winds and warm showers, with the promise of natural life renewed for all living things.

CHAPTER EIGHT

The Summer People

APRIL WAS usually alternately lovely and bleak. March was just bleak and May was just lovely. People showed more exasperation at March than any other month; they never knew how to dress. If they got into summer things, it invariably blew and rained icicles. If they kept to their woollens, the heavens burned blue, the sun burned golden, and sweat ran.

Jerrie came home, surprising her parents, one Friday night. She had to be back by Monday for classes. She'd made up the maths her appendectomy had interfered with, which pleased her, and she had a look of anxiety that showed something was bothering her other than scholastics. She told her mother she was going down to see Uncle Caleb and drove off. When John arrived home Madge told him where their daughter had gone. They looked at one another.

Jerrie didn't get home until late and the look of anxiety was gone. She came into the parlour where her parents habitually sat by the fire evenings and said, " Why didn't you tell me Frank was up here last winter?"

Her father put aside his book and soberly considered her cold-flushed, very pretty face. " It wasn't important," he said, watching her closely. " He's writing a book—or something like that."

" Mother; you could have asked him over for dinner. He's a terrible cook." Jerrie was smiling, but not whole-heartedly smiling.

Madge said, " Is he? I suppose most men are and all boys must be, darling."

" He's almost finished with the book," said Jerrie, going after a cup of coffee and calling back to them. " Can I bring you anything?"

Her parents declined the offer. Quietly, John said, " She must have had a long visit with him. I thought you said she was going—"

C

" The places adjoin, John. Anyway they *are* friends."

Jerrie returned, got close to the fire and said it was very cold out. They waited, knowing full well she hadn't exhausted the topic of Frank Levinsky yet. She hadn't.

" It's a beautiful novel. It's so—sensitive and perceptive. Someday Frank will be a prominent author. I wish you could read the manuscript."

" Is that what you did today, dear?" asked Madge.

" Part of it, yes. But it's quite long and Uncle Caleb and I had to get back."

" Caleb took you over there?"

Jerrie's short, curly hair danced when she shook her head at her mother. " The other way around. *I* took *him* over there, after he told me Frank was here." She returned to an earlier thought and stopped smiling. " Mother; I invited him to dinner tomorrow night. You should see the things he's been eating. It would be hilarious if it wasn't sad."

John considered the book in his lap. He knew his daughter. It was frequently said that mothers knew daughters and fathers knew sons. In this case, having no son and having a daughter who thought and reacted as he also did, John'd never had much difficulty understanding Jerrie.

He understood her now and, because he did, all those ghosts from last fall returned. She liked Frank Levinsky very much. It shone in her eyes, was audible in her words, even showed in her soft-tender smile when she mentioned his name. John sighed.

Later, in their upstairs bedroom John said something about his misgivings. Madge didn't refute them this time. She was not so old she hadn't also seen the signs, but she'd even seen some John hadn't seen at all. She said, "Why does love have to be blind?" and her husband whirled.

"Who said anything about love?"

"I just did, John."

Neither of them was sleepy although the bed was soft, the room warm, and beyond the storm-windows the night was frigidly gusty with dazzling white stars far, far away through a crystal-clear void. Ordinarily it would have been an ideal sleeping night. Jerrie had changed all that.

"I suppose we should have had him to dinner, John. After all he's just a boy."

John wasn't sure what being 'just a boy' had to do with it but he said, "He'll be here tomorrow night . . . I don't really know Frank very well . . . At the store, and now and then at the river or in town, but we've never talked."

"You'll have your chance to see him tomorrow night. Good night, love."

The following morning John had a little difficulty concentrating at the store, which was open every Saturday until noon. He was ready to toss it all up and lock the front door by ten but he hung on until noon before heading back home.

There was a light drizzle falling, not enough to do any good, just enough to be nasty. But if John had noticed, or had bothered to put a hand out, he'd have discovered that the soft rainfall was warm. That signalled the frost was past. There might still be a late frost, but winter was definitely gone.

The people with fruit trees now turned fervent. Some years, when the trees were all blossoming, a killing black frost set in silently at night. By morning every blossom was shrivelled brown and the buds were dead. That meant no fruit for that particular year.

Madge met John in the driveway with a request. They needed five pounds of sugar and a bottle of liquor. Neither were drinkers, not even very good social drinkers, but oftentimes guests liked a highball before dinner.

John backed the car out and went after the needed articles. At the grocery store he met his book-keeper, also shopping. She said she'd just heard that Meyer Levinsky was coming after Frank the very next day. She'd received that juicy bit of information from the Newport local telephone operator who manged to couple an avocational hunger for gossip to a vocational position as local Bell System employee.

" Furthermore," confided Emily in a very low voice, " Meyer Levinsky was angry. He wanted to know what was so hard about writing a book that Frank had to go sit in an icebox to write it, and maybe starve as well. He said Meyer Junior was overseas now and Frank's mother needed him with her, so he was coming after Frank."

John digested all this, wondered why Meyer hadn't just ordered Frank home since Frank had a car of his own, put it all out of his mind and headed homeward for the second time, with a bottle of Jack Daniels and a plastic sack of white sugar.

Jerrie floated down the stairs in something that was very easy on the eyes but was not in any sense formal. John, eyeing his daughter, thought that she had excellent taste in clothes and the figure to wear almost anything. She caught him looking, winked, then went to see if she could help her mother.

Frank arrived on time. In fact he might have been a little early. He had two bouquets, one for Jerrie, one for Madge. The mystery was where he'd got flowers without picking them himself. There was no flower shop in Newport.

He looked very presentable, which didn't exactly surprise John Leavitt, although he'd entertained some doubts for a while. Not that he'd ever seen Frank when he wasn't clean and presentable, but being a bachelor does something to any man, if he stays at it long enough.

John made polite conversation by asking after Frank's parents. They were moderately fine, said Frank. His mother had taken it rather hard when Meyer'd been ordered overseas with his mortar outfit. His father had been busy in the city, but then as he said, his father would manage to keep busy anywhere; Meyer Senior was one of those nerve-activated compulsive workers.

They discussed Frank's book, which he seemed more embarrassed about than pleased with. It was, exactly as he claimed, a first novel with all the nuances of most first novels, for although the plot was fair and the writing certainly better than many *published* authors' work, it still had that certain amateurishness to it Frank was working now at dispelling.

He didn't tell John the story nor the setting and John made no enquiries along those lines. He was in fact being very discreet respecting the novel, for it seemed to him that if Frank had wanted all that privacy for doing his writing, he'd also be reticent about delving very deeply into it, conversationally.

The young man was perfectly at ease, but for some

reason John couldn't quite define nor grapple with, there was a gulf between them. They made polite parlour conversation easily but neither man made any noticeable impression upon the other. John had an old pool table out in the garage but it was too late to suggest a game now. Madge and Jerrie were lugging things back and forth from kitchen to dining-room.

John asked when the rest of Frank's family would be up. He had nothing snide in mind. In fact, while he hadn't forgot what Emily Trotten had told him, he almost had.

Frank looked at his crossed legs. " Probably not until it gets too hot in the city. But—my father will be here tomorrow." The level, somewhat brooding eyes went to John's face and remained there. " He thinks writing books is a waste of time. He says it's fine for women but men should get into something solid like construction." Frank lopsidedly smiled. " I bought him some Hemingway. He'd have understood Hemingway, or Steinbeck. He didn't even open the book." Frank's crooked grin turned a little sardonic. " How do you get a point across to someone who won't see it?"

John said, " You just go on rowing your own canoe, I guess, Frank."

The younger man's eyes brightened towards John. " That's exactly what I did—what I've been doing this past winter. You've got wise answers, Mister Leavitt. I wish . . . Well, anyway; he's coming tomorrow to make me go home."

" Are you going?"

Frank nodded. " But not for the reason you think, Mister Leavitt. Not because I'm afraid of my father. My mother took it pretty hard when my brother went overseas."

" It happens every day, Frank."

" I know that. But you don't know my mother."

John said he could imagine, that mothers were all alike on some subjects. He then mentioned a drink. Frank declined with a broad smile. "My appetite's sharp enough, if it's all right with you, Mister Leavitt."

It was fine with John; he didn't want a drink, but if Frank had taken one then John'd have felt bound to drink with him.

Frank asked about the fire. John told him what he knew. Otherwise they didn't discuss the old church. They talked about Caleb, though, and both agreed he was getting too old to live out there on his acreage during the bad winters.

" But he'd fight hammer and tongs if anyone tried to move him," said John.

Frank told of having Caleb over for supper a few times until the old man, a lifelong bachelor, finally said he wasn't coming back any more unless Frank would let him do the cooking.

They laughed about that, so finally they found a common ground and got easy with one another. John recalled anecdotes about Caleb back when he'd been a boy and Frank told of Caleb's exasperation at trying to teach Frank and Meyer how to manage a boat, how to fish, how to eat food with a little sand in it.

By the time Madge and Jerrie came to join them, and rest a moment before they all went in to eat, Frank was laughing easily and John was smiling with a twinkle in his normally unsmiling New England eyes.

When they went into the dining-room it remained the same only with Jerrie taking part, and Madge also, to a lesser degree.

All in all it was a very pleasant evening. Of course the meal was excellent but then it had to be since Madge had made it. She was very gifted in many ways.

Later, when Frank had effusively thanked Madge and John for their hospitality, and had gone out on to the porch with Jerrie, Madge said she liked him. John had never felt different but he had misgivings on Jerrie's part.

She was much too young to be thinking of marriage. At least John told himself that, but if he'd been quite candid he'd have recalled that when he and Madge had been married they'd been the same age.

And of course there were the invisible insurmountables. Differences in heritage, in background, in total environments. People he thought, found marriage a difficult undertaking as the years passed; it was better if they weren't handed any unnecessary handicaps right at the start.

Madge offered a penny for his thoughts but he turned that aside with a smile and wink. " Bed time," he said. " They're going to freeze out there, but we don't have to."

" They're young," said his wife. " All right, come along John . . . ?"

" Yes?"

" What will happen if they are serious?"

" You're serious about everything at Jerrie's age, Madge, but she's sensible. They're too young. Besides, she wants to complete college."

Madge wasn't convinced. "I wanted to finish too, remember?"

CHAPTER NINE

The Advent of Spring

JERRIE LEFT very early. So early in fact her parents weren't aware of her departure until they drowsily heard her car cough to life down in the driveway while they were still abed.

Later, over hot coffee, they recapitulated the dinner. It had been pleasant, they conceded, Frank had proved well mannered, pleasant, with an excellent sense of humour.

But it was a relief that Jerrie'd returned to school.

The day turned warm, business at the emporium was brisk, and until almost eleven o'clock when Madge brought round some store-mail which had been inadvertently delivered at home, John scarcely had a breathing spell.

After Madge headed for the grocery store, John read the mail, looked up when a thick shadow fell across his line of vision, and turned to meet what he'd thought would be a customer. It was Meyer Levinsky.

"Good morning, Mister Leavitt. On my way to pick up Frank and take him back to the city. It's a little early for summer vacation."

C*

John nodded. Levinsky was casually dressed and looked fresh despite the long drive. He must have got up in the middle of the night to arrive in Newport before noon.

" Too bad about the old church," Levinsky said. " But at least that one's laid to rest, eh?"

John smiled. It was a practical way to look at it. For a while last summer he'd been fearful. Not that he'd feared a fight with Levinsky. He was a New Englander; they did not often run from trouble. But neither did they go out looking for it.

" Maybe there's something else," Levinsky said without much enthusiasm. " And maybe I was crazy even thinking of trying to work up something in Newport. Like my banker said, what's the point? You sink several thousand bucks into resort property and you won't live long enough to get back your six per cent, let alone your investment."

John might have disputed that but he didn't. All he said was: " The old-fashioned idea that resort property is a poor investment, based on a four-month holiday period, is becoming less and less valid, Mister Levinsky. But your banker was right on one thing: It's no way to get a fast return, but then New England has never qualified in that direction. Not for farmers or lumbermen, fishermen or storekeepers." John smiled. " It's been a long-term haul for all of us."

Levinsky nodded, looked round where clerks were waiting on customers, and remarked that Newport seemed busy enough even though the ' summer people ' hadn't arrived yet.

John could have answered that sharply, Levinsky left himself wide open for it, but John just laughed. " The ' summer people ' are important, all right, but Newport was here and thriving long before any 'summer people' ever showed up, and it would go right on if none ever came again. On a smaller scale, of course."

Levinsky fished for a smoke, lit up and studied John a moment before he said, warily choosing his words. "Mister Leavitt, I got a problem with Frank. Now don't misunderstand me; I think Newport's great. Otherwise would I have stuck so much money into that white elephant out along the river? You sure as hell can't sell anything like that estate of ours at anywhere near what you got into it. But what is there for 'summer people' in Newport after the holiday season ends?"

"Probably not very much," said John, "for 'summer people'."

"That's just my point. Listen; would you tell that to Frank? He don't listen to me. He's got this wild idea about being an author; about living up here year round and writing. Y'know, books, articles, stuff like that. Doing maybe some regional histories of New England. You ever hear a better way to starve?"

John shook his head. "I'd have no reason to tell Frank anything, Mister Levinsky. It's none of my business what he does."

"He'd listen to you. He's told me you're a smart man, Mister Leavitt. And of course there's your daughter."

John's smile died entirely. He kept Jerrie out of it by saying, "I could name a dozen very successful New England writers. They live here year round."

"Don't give me no exceptions, Mister Leavitt. Frank isn't a writer. Maybe he wants to be one but that don't make him one and as far as I can see he'll be years eking out even a subsistence living. Look; what can he do in a place like Newport in the wintertime; what does he know about selling firewood or running a business, or even keeping alive through one of your blizzards?"

"He'd get by, Mister Levinsky."

"You're sure? Tell me; how come you're defending my son, he's no native."

"He's a native if he wants to live here year round, Mister Levinsky. If I were you I'd give him the chance."

"You're not me," grumped Levinsky, putting out his smoke and looking accusingly at the ash-tray. "Meyer's gone overseas. His mother is alone. I'm gone most of the day with business."

"Mister Levinsky I'd give anything if my daughter could be fifteen again. But she won't be and I can't arrange it. She's got a life of her own. We used to spend long winter evenings playing parcheesi and making candy and I even taught her to play billiards. Well; that's all gone now. You can't tie them to you forever. You shouldn't even want to, I guess, but you *do* want to. I'm sorry to hear Meyer's been shipped out but I'd be a lot sorrier if you made Frank go back to the city just to keep your wife happy. Frank's twenty-two or three years old. Maybe he'll never be a writer but at least right now he's trying to be a man—on his own."

Levinsky's thin lips drooped. "A man he can be in my business, Mister Leavitt."

"Evidently he doesn't want to be a man in your business. Evidently he wants to try it up here on his own as a writer. If he falls flat at least he's tried something—anything—on his own. That's more important to a kid his age, right now, than success."

Levinsky shrugged. "You're quite a philosopher,

Mister Leavitt," he said, and nodded. "Be back in a couple of months when the weather warms up."

John stood a while after the other man's departure wondering why he'd been so bold. Normally, he kept strictly out of other folks' affairs. Miss Emily came out to have him examine the previous month's slow accounts. He saw no names he didn't trust and told her so, knowing perfectly well what she'd do when she sent out the over-due statements; pen some of her little notes.

He had a Selectmen's meeting that night so as soon as the shadows began falling he left for home. His clerks would remain until five, then lock the place up.

There was a letter from Jerrie when he got home. Madge read it to him. Their daughter had caught up all around on her academic work and was cruising along now, as she put it, waiting for spring vacation to arrive, along with the end of the college term. She was confident. She also asked about Frank, about Caleb, about some of their older friends and relations, then closed with the suggestion that, if her budget would permit, she might drive home the following week-end.

"When you answer," John told Madge, "you might mention Frank's father came for him. That just might help her budget stretch until vacation. There'd be little reason for to drive home."

Along towards the end of April the weather modified; the days continued warm without being hot, flowers began to flourish, trees promised to bud soon, the sap was running and those white-birch patches on the mountainsides looked very white in the glowing dark, very dark green, of the spruce and pines and firs.

Ten days into May and the first adventuresome

' summer people ' appeared. These were usually the same people; fishermen mostly, come north to get in on the tail-end of the salmon runs. Normally, holidaymakers didn't appear until the end of May or the first of June.

It didn't really help the local economy much; there weren't enough ' summer people ' to do that, although they did noticeably swell the population, and of course the wintertime period of insularity was broken by their trickling influx, which was viewed as the forerunner of what would come within the next four or five weeks.

John was out back checking-in merchandise from an enormous truck-tractor—his usual stocking up for the first summer-trade run—and only turned to enter the store after a solid hour of supervising the off-loading, when he saw Frank Levinsky leaning back there against the loading-dock doorway gazing impassively at all the disarray the off-loading had made. John was surprised. " Well hello, Frank," he said stepping over where the tall, quiet young man stood. " You're up early, aren't you?"

Frank's blue eyes showed mild surprise. " I never left, Mister Leavitt," he said. " I've been here all winter."

It was John's turn to show surprise. " I thought, when your father came up a month or so ago . . ."

" No. I didn't go back with him. We had a long talk, then he went back alone."

" Oh." John considered the sheaf of manifests in his hand. " Well; what can I do for you?"

" I need a job, Mister Leavitt."

That caught John unprepared too. " A job? What kind of a job?"

" Well; unloading trucks I guess, or clerking, or anything at all."

John always increased his labour force after June with at least two temporary clerks in the store, but it was a trifle early yet for that. He said, " Have you tried elsewhere? Perhaps down at the drug store, or over at the feed store?"

Frank shook his head. " I just drove into town a few minutes ago. I thought I'd ask you first."

John procrastinated. " Come on into the office, Frank. I've got to give these manifests to Miss Emily. There's a percolator of coffee in there."

Miss Emily nodded, a trifle stiffly, when Frank Levinsky trailed in after Miss Emily's employer. She went right on working at her desk as though neither man existed. John handed her the papers. She dumped them into a wire basket without a glance.

They had a cup of coffee, Frank saying nothing, John in an uneasy quandary. " It's a little early for hiring summer help," he said, swishing his coffee and trying to come to a decision. " Frank; I don't want to get in the middle in any family disputes."

Frank smiled. " There's no dispute, Mister Leavitt. In fact that's why I thought of you on the way into town this morning. My father told me he'd seen you before he came out to the place. He didn't tell me what you said, but it must have made an impression. Dad just asked me if I couldn't do my writing at home in the city. I told him I couldn't. He then asked if I had enough money to get me through, then we fried some steaks—he's a better cook than I am—then he left, after we talked for a while. He mentioned speaking to you. I've been wondering what you told him, Mister Leavitt."

John finished his coffee, looked at Miss Emily, who

was entering figures in a large ledger, still oblivious to
their presence. She'd of course developed the knack of
total concentration over the years. He asked if Frank
would care for a second cup of coffee, and when Frank
declined he made his decision. "Go see what else you
can find around town, son, then come back after lunch
and maybe I'll have worked out something."

Frank left.

Miss Emily, putting up the ledger, sat down to flick
through the manifests as she said, "You could use the
boy, Mister Leavitt. I think he'd be a worker too—even
if he is—well—summer people."

There were complications that Miss Emily had either
purposely overlooked or neglected to mention. Not actually serious complications, but nevertheless things John
preferred not to get involved in. One of them was having
anyone working in the store his daughter was interested
in. Another was Meyer Levinsky's reaction to having his
son clerking in John Leavitt's store.

He went home for a late lunch, talked it over with
Madge, returned to the store and at two o'clock, when
Frank returned, John hired him.

The salary was not large, but as John pointed out,
until business picked up the following month, the result
of returning holidaymakers he could scarcely afford to
pay more.

Frank accepted and offered to remove his jacket and
go to work at once. John smiled at that. "Tomorrow will
be soon enough."

That evening at home, when Madge told him she was
writing to Jerrie, John said without much enthusiasm,
she might as well tell their daughter Frank Levinsky was

now working at the emporium for her father.

John had no doubts about either Frank's ability or willingness. But he had that uneasy feeling one gets about hiring a questionable person. The feeling persisted even when old Caleb showed up the following afternoon to say he'd thought John had done a wise thing, hiring the lad. Caleb didn't say *why* it'd been a wise thing, but then John was supposed to know that without having it pointed out to him, evidently.

CHAPTER TEN

A Parcel of Tax-Deeded Land

JUNE WAS a busy month. Realtors, who'd sold not a stick throughout the winter, had their shingles up again, were seen taking prospective purchasers into the countryside almost every day, and of course the 'summer people' came straggling in. Most were people who owned estates or cottages, or just A-frame cabins throughout the countryside. The river hadn't warmed up yet and if one cared to make the effort—which no one did—there was still visible snow in the high country farther back where

the spine of New England's granite chain of mountains
stood eternal and sharp-limned against the azure skies,
waiting to be explored.

The ski enthusiasts became boating enthusiasts. This
was what John Leavitt'd had in mind that day he'd told
Meyer Levinsky it was no longer valid to say Newport
was only a summertime town. It *had* been such a place
for many years, since John had been a young boy, in
fact, but now, with the ski-ing fever rivalling the holiday-
fever of summertime fishing and boating, Newport seemed
on the verge of becoming a year-round playground.

Whether the natives would take kindly to having their
winters as well as summers interrupted was problematical,
but that wasn't likely to change anything since the moun-
tain slopes were a natural place for skiers.

The afternoon Jerrie arrived home her father was out
back with Frank checking off freshly arrived cases of
merchandise, and Frank made a remark that stuck in
John's head long afterwards. Speaking of the change in
Newport young Frank said, " I'm not so sure it's simply
that the city isn't too distant, or that the ski slopes happen
to be ideal, nor even that the river is indispensable. I
think it may have even more to do with the population
increase, Mister Leavitt. Where New York City once had
a two-million population it now has nearly double that,
with all the rest of the country growing and expanding
proportionately."

Frank was a thinker, John discovered. He wasn't as
ebullient as Meyer Junior, nor as blunt and practical as
Meyer Senior. John didn't know Mrs. Levinsky at all
so couldn't attribute Frank's quiet thoughtfulness to her,
but he was certain of one thing; it had been a good day

for him, and the store, the day he'd hired Frank Levinsky.

The natives came in time to accept Frank. Some even asked for him when they came to the emporium. It was uncanny too, for despite what Frank's father had said about his son's inability to work with his hands, Frank always came up with the right answers to questions customers asked about fishing gear, plumbing supplies, even guns and ammunition.

John discovered quite accidentally how Frank acquired this knowledge the day he agreed to put in a line of good—and expensive—outboard motors. Frank took all the literature home with him that night and the following day in the most casual way got into a technical discussion with the salesman which afterwards inclined the salesman to tell John he was lucky to have among his clerks one who'd had experience with the new line of motors.

Frank and John went to lunch late that same day. John repeated what the salesman had said and Frank smiled. " Nothing very complicated, Mister Leavitt. If we're to sell those motors then someone in the store ought to be able to talk about them."

John told Madge and would have also told Jerrie, but she'd already driven off, or, as John called it, referring to her rough-riding little foreign car, she'd " saddled up."

In mid-June the Levinskys came for the summer. John diplomatically asked if perhaps Frank didn't think he should stop working and spend the time with his parents. He gave John a long, slow look.

" If you think I should," he said, standing there waiting for what John interpreted to be a look of disapproval.

" *I'd* rather you stayed on," he told the younger man.
" I was just thinking of—other things, Frank."

" My mother, Mister Leavitt?"

" Well, yes."

" It wouldn't be good for either of us. I'd rather work here, if it's all right with you."

It was all right; in fact it was more than just ' all right '. Frank had mastered the entire business faster than anyone else who'd ever worked for John. He even made decisions for customers, which was a risky business even for John, who knew both his merchandise and his customers, and there hadn't been a single complaint.

The fact that Frank and Jerrie were ' going steady ' as folks observed around town, didn't enter into the working agreement between Frank and John Leavitt, although one evening when John mentioned at supper he thought Jerrie also ought to go out with some of the other boys in Newport, she said there were no other boys as mature, and John silently had to agree.

Then Meyer Levinsky came to the store one warm morning and handed John a crisp paper, complete with notary seal and tax-stamps. Meyer didn't say a thing. He lit a cigarette while he waited for John to finish studying the paper, and was quietly watching the other man's face when John suddenly turned.

" It's a deed, Mister Levinsky, to that parcel of ground where the old church used to stand."

Levinsky nodded, smoke curling up past one squinted pale eye. " Got it over at the tax collector's office at the county seat, Mister Leavitt. Got it yesterday afternoon."

" I don't see how," murmured John, looking again at

the Grant Deed to see whether or not it had been officially recorded. It had. Meyer Levinsky would henceforth be carried on the tax-rolls as owner in fee-simple of the land described on the deed.

" Well, it wasn't very difficult. But first I brought that thing round for you to see. My reason? I know there was opposition last year while the church still stood. I wanted to know, first, and everyone else, second, that I did *not* work any shenanigans to acquire that piece of property. I didn't even know it was on the roll of delinquent-tax parcels until I got to looking over the other parcels. I don't want people saying Meyer Levinsky pulled some shyster stunt to get that land none of the natives wanted him to have."

John put down the paper. Someone had made a terrible error; the township of Newport hadn't paid the taxes for almost six years, which automatically put the parcel of land up for sale on a redemption basis. John, for one, never bothered reading the legally required newspaper lists of to-be-sold bits of local land. Evidently no one else had either, or someone surely would have brought this condition to the attention of the Selectmen. No one had, Levinsky had seen the delinquency, had paid cash for redemption, and now was legal owner.

Levinsky said. " I'd still like to build the discothéque." He said it mildly. " Of course I'll need a building permit. And of course, too, if the Selectmen want to, they can side-track my application or find fault with my blueprints, or just plain refuse the building permit. That's what I'm here today to ask you about. I'm not going to build anything on that piece of ground without local approval. I know all about harassment, Mister Leavitt.

There's not enough in this thing for me up here, to fight for."

John was still stunned. All he said was, " There'll be another meeting next week. Your application to build will come up then."

" And this time—tell me—will I get a straight answer, yes or no?"

John nodded. " I think you will. This time." He knew very well Levinsky would get his answer. He also knew the other Selectmen would be as surprised as he was that the old church-site had passed out of their control without them knowing anything about it. He did *not* think either Charley or Ed, his fellow Selectmen, were going to believe Levinsky hadn't deliberately bought that piece of ground, knowing all the time it was going to come up for redemption on the open market.

Of course, under the law, there was a year of grace for the former owners to come up with a cash settlement, plus interest, plus full reimbursement for whoever'd bought the land at tax sale, plus cash value for whatever improvements the new owner had put upon the premises— in this case no improvements at all. And John had a bad feeling the banker was going to roar penurious protest to those charges, plus an expenditure of cash from a chronically empty township treasury, while at the same time fiercely denouncing Meyer Levinsky for sliding in behind everyone's back and purchasing the old church-site.

In fact for the next two days John was preoccupied with the dilemma he saw in the making, and without his being aware of it, Frank took over more and more responsibility in the store. John had a long talk with Jeremy Benson, the lawyer whose office was above the

bank, concerning alternatives to outright abandonment
of that piece of land. Old Jeremy was emphatic. He was
also slightly caustic, pointing out that it was part of the
specific duties of the Selectmen to watch over township
property, which in this case they most certainly had
flagrantly neglected to do.

" But unless the town wants to buy that piece of ground
back and is willing to make the full cash settlement, John,
plus penalties. I'm afraid Mister Levinsky just might get
his damned coffee-house."

Jeremy slyly smiled. " You could procrastinate on the
building permit, you know."

John had already opposed that course when it'd come
up once before. " I'd rather have an honest decision," he
told old Benson.

The lawyer was indifferent. " Well; if Levinsky would
sell it back to the town, perhaps on instalments so's we
could pay for it as revenue accrued . . ." Benson threw
up his hands. " John; what in the hell do we want with
that ground anyway? No one's going to build another
church there—not right smack-dab in the centre of town
where all you've got around it are stores and warehouses.
Not even parking space if people would drive into town
for Sunday services. I'd favour letting him keep the
damned thing. Build his fancy coffee-house if he wants.
At least the city'd get licensing and tax money from his—
discothéque, or whatever he calls that thing."

John stood by the door gazing back at old Benson.
" You're forgetting something, Jeremy. That also happens
to be the oldest cemetery in Newport."

Back at the store Miss Emily said Madge had called,
then Charley Hudson had called from the bank, and that

Ed Smith had called from his plumbing shop on the northerly outskirts of town.

Miss Emily also studied John's expression as he crossed the office and sank down behind his desk. But she was a taciturn, discreet woman; blunt as a dull knife when the occasion arose, but nonetheless discreet. So all she said was: " It'll have to do with the old church-site, won't it, Mister Leavitt?" After thirty years she still doggedly refused to call him John, nor to permit herself to be addressed any more familiarly than *Miss* Emily.

John looked over. " Don't tell me it's all over town so soon?"

" Of course, Mister Leavitt; you didn't expect something like *that* to be kept a secret, did you?"

Not a secret exactly, he told her, but he'd hoped it might remain quietly out of the common knowledge until he'd had a chance to come up with some kind of solution —which, at present anyway, it did not look like he nor anyone else was going to come up with.

Frank came in to interrupt their little talk with three hire-purchase contracts for John to approve—or disapprove—each one made out to a different person for the purchase of those new outboard boat motors.

John scanned the signatures and approved each one. " Old customers," he murmured, handing back the papers. " Make the terms to suit them, Frank. And Frank —you sold those three motors just today?"

The blue eyes laughed back. " Just today," said Frank and left the office with two sets of eyes on him. Miss Emily almost smiled. *Almost*. " I told you, Mister Leavitt, I told you. That young man'll be running the store in another year or two—unless he decides to . . ." Miss

Emily looked suddenly startled at herself, looked swiftly down at the ledger in front of her and became very busy all of a sudden.

"Unless he decides to get married and leave," John said, finishing it for her, and went to get himself a cup of coffee.

Five o'clock seemed to take forever to come around on this day. The newspaper telephoned at four and John violently shook his head at Miss Emily when she answered the thing. She said John was too busy to be bothered at the moment and rang off. Then she looked straight at him and shook her head.

"I wouldn't want to be a Selectman right now, Mister Leavitt. Not until this mess is straightened out once and for all. Tempers'll be running high again."

CHAPTER ELEVEN

Choosing Sides

TEMPERS RAN high right enough. For the first time in many months when the Selectmen met the following mid-week people filled the chairs of the meeting room. Even old Caleb was there, looking more frail than ever, but also looking very alert and watchful.

The banker morosely went through the motions of bringing up all the small matters on the agenda—that previously denied request for more money for the police force, the matter of the town dump, an unsightly place which needed a fresh hole dug and the old hole covered up, a question of the legality of Newport's leash-law covering dogs running loose in town. Then, the last thing to be considered—building permits.

This ordinarily was not much of a job, although each June and July the number of applications seemed to increase noticeably over the previous requests. Also, since there was an immense township map on one wall, it was never very difficult to ascertain exactly where each potential builder proposed to erect his new cottage or home, or simple A-frame structure.

It took three-quarters of an hour to work through the applications, with John reading them off and Charley over at the map with Ed tracing out the precise location each time.

There were no applications to build within the actual confines of the town, except one, and John put that one aside. He'd already seen Meyer Levinsky and Frank among the spectators. Finally, when all the other permits had been approved—barring one made by a man who stated it as his intention to tie into the city water system, which he could not do for the simple reason that city water mains did not extend as far out as his cabin-site —the single remaining permit lay alone in front of John.

He read off the name and gave the legal description of the property. No one went over to the wall-map. No one even looked round at it. The banker's neck reddened and Ed Smith picked up the pencil and wrote something on the pad in front of himself. They were leaving it up to John to institute action. He did.

"I propose that we decide tonight what action should be taken on this application."

The banker looked over at him sternly. "It will take time to look into this matter," he said.

Ed the plumber nodded agreement.

John took a deep breath. "The same application was made last summer. We asked for time to study it then. The only thing that's changed since then is that the old church burned down."

The banker's stern look turned hostile. "All right; if you are willing to move for immediate action I am prepared to cast my vote."

John knew how this was going to go. He also knew the silent spectators were going to speak up very soon now. He asked for the vote. Ed Smith voted against the application. Charley Hudson voted against it. John sat loosely looking across the table at them. "The one consideration I'm worried about," he said, not yet willing to cast his vote—which wouldn't make much difference anyway—"concerns the old graves in the little cemetery behind where the old church used to stand."

The first interruption came. Meyer Levinsky arose.

"Gentlemen! I am Meyer Levinsky, owner of that piece of ground and supplicant on that application for permission to build a discothéque on that ground."

John nodded, mildly surprised at Levinsky's grammar, which was correct thus far while it normally was not.

"Proceed, Mister Levinsky," he said.

"Gentlemen: I propose moving the old cemetery."

There was an audible gasp throughout the crowded room. Levinsky ignored that.

"I have three sites to offer, all three of which I've acquired over the past three years, each one five times as large as the present cemetery, each one far enough out so that the encroachment cannot possibly occur for many years—and each one ideal in all the ways a cemetery should be."

Charley Hudson sat like a bulldog glaring from slitted eyes at Levinsky. Ed Smith was watching him too, but with a more caustic and hostile expression. Ed seemed ready to spring to his feet and denounce Levinsky. Charley seemed prepared merely to sit there and chop down every suggestion Levinsky made.

"These sites," said Levinsky, "have cost me a lot more money than the church-site." He paused, looked into the upturned faces on all sides then said, "I'll give the town its pick of those sites. I'll *give* the town whichever site it chooses, and . . ." he paused for another look around, " and, I'll pay the expenses of having those graves properly and technically moved. I thank you." Levinsky sat down.

A slow whisper swept through the chambers like a low wind. John tried to guess from looking at the faces what local reaction had been.

Charley Hudson said, looking straight over to where Meyer Levinsky sat, "It's not the duty of this Board, Mister Levinsky, to pass judgement on either the moral or ethical probity of such a move. We cannot arbitrarily pass any ordinance respecting those graves out there."

Levinsky stood up at once, slightly red in the face. "Who can, if you can't?"

Charley was ready for that. Evidently all the time Levinsky had been speaking Hudson had been devising his ploy. Now he gave it bluntly back to Levinsky.

"Only the people whose father and forefathers are buried there. In other words, Mister Levinsky," said Charley, with an almost sneering emphasis on the 'Mister', "we'll have to run down a good many descendants of those people—some of whom were buried there over a hundred years ago and whose names are no longer carried on city or county tax-rolls as residents —secure their permission, then, granting that the descendants of those buried there who are with us yet will agree, then we can take action towards voting on your application."

Charley was right, John knew, but that wasn't what Charley cared about, and John also knew that; he wanted to stall Meyer Levinsky indefinitely and it looked very much as though he'd just discovered the perfect way of doing it.

Again that soft sigh of sound passed over the big room. People were watching Meyer Levinsky and his son. They both sat rigidly gazing down at the Selectmen. Levinsky's face grew redder. He got slowly to his feet, looked round the room, then addressing Charley Hudson, said, "Gentlemen: I appreciate your concern. That's why I've gone to the expense of locating better sites for your cemetery. I respect the dead. That's why I've taken the time and effort to find out about trained people to do the removing. But . . ." he looked hard at Charley Hudson. "But, I think I'm showing more concern for your forefathers than you show. It looks that way to me, since none of you cared enough about their graves to keep that piece of property from going under the hammer at a tax-sale."

Levinsky sat down, fished for a cigar, ground it between his teeth without lighting it, and looked neither to the right nor left.

This time the sigh of sound was lower, as though there were some growls of indignation. Charley Hudson swung back to the pad in front of him on the table. He shot a smoky look at John, not openly hostile but not overly friendly either. Ed Smith kept his face frozen. He was under the intent scrutiny of half the people in the silent room.

John said, speaking clearly but quietly, " I vote in favour of Mister Levinsky's application to build."

It was like dropping a grenade. People yanked straight up in their chairs. Voices rose to a steady buzzing hum. Charley Hudson smiled a cold, ferocious smile and rolled up his eyes indicating to John that Charley thought John had just destroyed himself not only as a Selectman but perhaps as a merchant also.

Jeremy Benson stood up, back near the door and went unnoticed until he spoke over the hum, asking permission to be heard. Everyone looked back. Old Benson was known locally as somewhat of a Philistine. He'd been outspokenly iconoclastic more than once. John along with everyone else squirmed a little.

" It seems to me, gentlemen," said the lawyer, looking straight down at the Selectmen, " that Mister Levinsky has been very fair. It also seems to me Mister Hudson has made a good point—about getting permission from the descendants of those dead people to move the graves. But I think there are precedents in the law to cover exigencies where no descendants can be found, and unless I'm very incorrect in my assumption—which I'll check in the law library over at the county seat tomorrow—after reasonable efforts have been made to locate those descendants and have proven unavailing, then it lies within the purview of our elected Selectmen to decide whether or not the cemetery should be moved—in the best interests of the town. Thank you."

Jeremy sat down. Charley Hudson was doodling furiously on his pad of paper. He had only once looked up. That had been when Benson had asked to be recognised. Now, Charley's thick red neck was very red, his lips were pursed, and his lowered eyes were smouldering slits.

Ed Smith said, " It all boils down to more study, more thought and, since we only meet once a month, I'd like to suggest we declare this meeting at an end, and use the next thirty days coming to a decision.

John was whipped and knew it. He acceded, the meeting was declared ended and people began quietly to shuffle out. Charley raised up, watched the mumbling spectators squeezing through the doorway, swung back and said, " John; you couldn't have got a decision tonight no matter what happened."

John shrugged. He was convinced of that although he hadn't been convinced earlier.

Charley then leaned forward and quietly said, " Don't take up for Levinsky, John. We're not going to have some city-type joint in Newport as long as I can actively stop it. If you defend the man and try to swing opinion in his favour I'll block you right down the line."

John's eyes rose to Hudson's face and stayed there. He felt anger stirring. " A threat, Charley?" he asked.

Hudson's thick shoulders rose and fell. He did not answer. But he smiled again, that wolfish, fierce little smile.

"You just got yourself an opponent, Charley. You just assured it. You ought to know by now I don't scare worth a damn. You aused to try bullying me in school and it didn't work then either."

The large room was almost empty now. Ed Smith, looking anxious, said, "Cut it out, you two. Don't let's get to fighting among ourselves. The only way we're ever going to come out of this is to stick together. If Levinsky gets us divided . . ." Ed rolled his eyes and let out a big sigh.

John stood up, still simmering with slow anger. Across the table Charley also arose, but Charley kept his head lowered while he tore the first page off his tablet and crumpled it in one big meaty hand.

Ed Smith was the last one to leave the chamber. He dutifully switched off the lights, closed and locked the double-hung doors, and marched down the steps out into the warm, lovely night where little bunches of people were scattered, heatedly discussing what had transpired upstairs.

John found his wife and daughter waiting, which surprised him since he hadn't spotted them among the spectators. Madge smiled up at him with visible worry in her eyes.

"Charley didn't like you coming out in favour, John," she said. "Ed didn't either."

He took both wife and daughter by an arm and started down towards the store where his car was parked. "I can't help what Ed and Charley liked, Madge. I have to do and say what *John Leavitt* likes."

Jerrie was quiet until they were in the car heading homeward, then she burst out with a fierce protest. "Mister Levinsky bent over backwards, Dad. He didn't have to offer that ground nor agree to stand all the expense of moving those graves—did he?"

John didn't know. He didn't think so, but all he said was, "Honey; Mister Benson'll be able to answer those questions better than I will."

"But didn't it seem fair to you, what he offered?"

"Yes, it seemed fair, Jerrie. But it's not altogether a matter of fairness. It's also a matter of emotion. People aren't going to be entirely rational about this. It's not like Newport isn't already antagonistic towards 'summer people'."

They said no more until they were in the kitchen at home with Madge making a pot of coffee. John sat at the kitchen table looking at his daughter. He smiled tiredly up at her. "Most rebels don't have very good causes these days, Jerrie. I think tonight you found a real one. That's what you want, isn't it?"

Jerrie looked steadily at her father. "I'm sorry, Dad," she said softly. "I didn't particularly want one—but I was handed one tonight anyway." She kissed his cheek. "Friends, anyway?"

He laughed. "Friends anyway."

D

CHAPTER TWELVE

Old Caleb was Right

THE FOLLOWING morning at breakfast Madge said,
" John; why did Jerrie act like you two were on opposite
sides last night? It seems to me you're both in favour
of the same thing."

John had thought on that before falling asleep the
night before. It seemed to him that while they both did
in fact favour Levinsky's plan, they did so for diferent
reasons and on different grounds. He said, " I am not
emotionally involved, Madge. I simply want what I think
is best for the town. Jerrie—well—I think Jerrie's got
different reasons, and if my hunch is right, even if I make
my point with the Selectmen, it's still going to be too slow,
too pragmatic, for Jerrie."

He wondered about Frank, too, but when he arrived
at the store Frank was as quietly business-like as ever. He
was pleasant without mentioning what had occurred the
night before, which was fine with John, who did not very
often mix his social or civic life with his business activi-
ties.

As for Charley's prediction that John would hurt himself professionally by his stand on the Levinsky matter,
it did not seem valid that day although more than once
customers stopped to discuss things and always worked

round to what had transpired last night. Some were neutral but most were not. Only one lectured John and that was a stiff-backed elderly woman. He did not argue.

Emily Trotten said nothing at all. She'd been among the spectators at the Selectmen's chambers. John had seen her sitting up there looking as prim and acid as always.

Ed came round in the afternoon to get a price on a carload of soil-pipe. He'd bid on a school construction job at Beaver Falls and had got it. It would be big enough to keep him occupied for the balance of the summer and he also said it probably would keep him out of town for a lot of the time.

John got the lists and as they went over them Ed relaxed a little until, just before he agreed on the purchase, he said, " Why don't you just leave sleepin' dogs lie, John? Let that damned cemetery sit in the middle of town, what difference does it make?"

" Ed; the town's grown up around that piece of ground. Sooner or later we're going to be pressured into moving it. What town can afford to have a crumbling old cemetery smack-dab in the middle of the business district?"

" Okay," agreed Ed placatingly, " but let's wait until folks make us move it."

" No. Levinsky has offered to do the whole job at no cost to the town, right now. If we wait another four or five years we'll have to move it anyway, then it'll cost a fortune."

Ed sighed. " Charley was mad last night," he murmured, as though reminding John of Charley's threat. " And, like I said, if Levinsky drives a wedge between us, we're goners. How'll we look to the people if we can't even agree among ourselves on this silly matter?"

"There's no law says we always have to agree on things, Ed." John closed the wholesale catalogues. "I'll telephone in your order this morning."

Ed shook his head slowly. "Forget the order, John," he said and walked out of the store.

That afternoon John got another jolt. Emil Franzen came in grim-faced, went to the office and asked Miss Emily for his monthly statement. Miss Emily said it wasn't current and wouldn't be until it was time to send out the monthly bills. Emil said he wanted it made out right now so he could pay it off. He said he had no intention of doing any more business with John Leavitt's store.

In a way that was ironic. Emil had come to Newport as a child. His parents had spoken broken English. Emil was considered a native but actually he probably had less personal involvement in historic or traditional Newport than anyone else who lived there, including the Levinskys who were at least third-generation Americans.

Miss Emily got indignant over that but she kept her temper until she'd made out the bill and handed it to Franzen, then she said. "Emil; you're not helping this thing any."

The old farmer, a sturdy, bull-necked and red-faced man, said severely, "Miss Emily; you mind your affairs and I'll mind mine. Summer people got no right pushin' everything around to suit them. The folk who've lived here all their lives got just as many rights."

Emil stalked out of the store about the time John came in from the loading-dock, saw Miss Emily standing stiff as a ramrod in the office doorway and walked over to her. She told him what had happened.

A place like Leavitt's emporium which did most of its business with natives and very little with summer people could be hurt. John had no illusions about that. On the other hand he was not a poor man; aside from the respectable competence he'd inherited from his father, he'd also banked a considerable sum on his own. He could go on operating the store for many years if it just broke even, but he didn't think of that in the days that followed; he thought instead of the friends he'd lose. Mostly, they were people he'd known all his life, had grown up with, had gone to school with. Some he was even related to.

Jerrie came round for Frank one evening at closing time. They were going swimming down by Caleb Adams' place where there was a fine little stretch of white beach. There'd be some other young people along too. She came into the office where her father and Miss Emily were drinking coffee and quietly discussing the day's receipts. It was the quiet, sundown time of day.

"I just got cut dead on the sidewalk by a girl I grew up with," she announced, and smiled cheerfully, almost truculently, at her father and Miss Emily. "I guess the war Uncle Caleb predicted last summer is now declared."

She told them what old Caleb had said the year before. Miss Emily sniffed. "That's very dramatic but anyone could have predicted there'd eventually be some kind of disagreement between *us* and *them*."

"The point is," said Jerrie, losing her smile and looking straight at Miss Emily, "there isn't any real difference, Miss Emily. *We* live differently than *they* do, but we're all the same people. Like farm people and town people. Or fishermen and woodsmen. Or storekeepers and factory workers. We make our living differently, we live in different type homes, but we're the same people."

John made no comment but he thought that sounded like something Frank might have said. He broke up the visit by suggesting she go get Frank before he drove off not knowing she was in the building. "He'll be out back locking the storehouse," her father said, "And Jerrie— I'm sorry about what happened on the sidewalk."

She kissed him on the cheek and departed.

Miss Emily went after her coat and hat on the ancient cloak-rack in the dark corner of the office. She turned and said, "It's a fine idea, Mister Leavitt, us being all the same people but with different ways of living. The trouble is—I don't think *us* or *them* is going to put a bit of store by it. Good night."

"Good night, Miss Emily."

Madge's day had been much better. She said the Community Garden Club, of which she was secretary, had decided to beautify the library grounds. They'd been over at Beaver Falls all day selecting the right shrubs and flowering plants. They'd also had to pay a visit to the county courthouse and get written permission from the County Clerk, who had charge of county buildings. He'd been very pleasant and helpful.

John made himself a highball of whisky and water. He was not a man who ordinarily drank a highball even when he'd had a strenuous day. Madge watched from the corner of her eye, then decided she'd join him. They went out back under the big tree and sat in the lawn-chairs.

He told her all that had happened. He did not mention his forebodings about business at the store. He didn't have to; Madge was smart enough woman despite her durable beauty.

She said, " Well; now that you brought it up, I did get a couple of little digs today. Nothing very pointed, just comments on the sanctity of the old cemetery."

" We're going to have to move it someday, Madge, and this way it'll cost the town nothing."

" I know, dear."

He looked at her remembering what Ed had said. " If we do nothing now, sooner or later we're going to have to move it anyway, then it'll cost like hell and Newport's town treasury never has any money in it. That'll mean a new tax—a cemetery tax. People scream even louder when that comes up."

Madge had to dash inside to check on dinner. When she came back she said Meyer Levinsky had called and wanted to see John tomorrow morning at the store. He shrugged. He didn't particularly wish to see Levinsky. And *not* in the store where customers would see them talking together—and draw incorrect inferences. But he didn't say anything.

Later, over a dinner for two, they discussed Jerrie. " She's happier than I've seen her since before the appendectomy," her mother said, and softly smiled. " I think you hit it on the head last night when you said she was a rebel with a cause."

" We haven't had one in the family in two hundred years, Madge. I think the last one would have been great-grandfather Leavitt who fought the British at Ticonderoga and Freeman's Farm and Bemis Heights."

They were sitting by the fireplace—unlit because of the warm night—when Charley Hudson came to the door looking grim and dogged. He was courtly towards Madge, whom he'd courted ardently in high-school but had lost to John, and distantly affable to John when Madge brought him into the parlour. She then excused herself to clean up the dinner dishes, leaving Charley facing John across the width of the large old-fieldstone fireplace.

Charley was never very diplomatic. He could upon occasion be tactful, but he didn't often bother with that either, except tonight when he began by saying, " John; it's been bothering me a little, this difference between us. Mind you I'm not afraid of a fight with you, but I somehow don't cotton to the idea. Not now; not this late in life. What I'd like to do is go over our differences on the Levinsky matter and see if we can't reach some kind of compromise."

John was agreeable and said so, but he also said he didn't see how they could possibly compromise on the basic issues because they were just too far apart. He then reiterated his position and explained why: " It will cost a lot of money, Charley, when we eventually have to move that cemetery at own expense. We'll have to impose a new tax."

Charley growled about that, understandably. " I've had all the new taxes I want," he said. " And old taxes too, for that matter. But it's Levinsky, John; I don't propose to see a man like that come in here and start throwing his weight around."

John was thoughtful while he listened. With Charley it was less the cemetery and more the man. He was emotional about this thing. John knew from long experience there was no way to discuss things sanely with someone who was operating on instinct, on emotion, alone.

He said, " Charley; you're not the only one who has folks buried up there. I'm perfectly willing to let them move my folks."

Hudson turned that aside with a short comment. " The dead are dead, John. It's not that."

"Last night before the people you made out that it was, Charley."

"Forget last night. I got mad. But Levinsky's trying to move in. I've read what the newspapers say about those Frenchified coffee-houses. They're a danger to local morality, John."

It was like trying to reason with a squirrel that jumped back and forth while you talked to it. Charley used anything he could think of as a reason for taking his obdurate stand but all the time it was Meyer Levinsky he really opposed. Yet each time John tried to bring it down to just Levinsky, Charley'd jump to another limb.

Madge came in an hour later and brought them coffee. Otherwise nothing came of the discussion and John hadn't expected anything to come of it.

Finally, just before Charley left, he revealed what John felt certain was his main reason in coming by. " Damned fools are taking sides, John. We've had four savings accounts closed out at the bank today. Now stuff like that won't look good in the stockholders' annual report."

John smiled. " I lost a big order from Ed today," he confessed, " and Emil paid up and walked out too."

" Then for God's sake let's work this out so's we see to an eye on it, or the whole blessed town's going to choose sides."

" It already has taken sides, Charley. By next week we'll all know where we stand."

D*

" You won't try, John?"

" You know damned well I'll try, Charley. But trying may not be enough. I won't change my stand and I doubt if you will." John pushed out his hand at the door. " But I'm glad you came by anyway."

Hudson shook and departed. Madge said, " I haven't seen him that upset in fifteen years."

John kissed her. " Let's turn in. I feel much better knowing he's lost a few accounts too."

CHAPTER THIRTEEN

Like A—Democrat!

MEYER LEVINSKY was dressed in suntan trousers and a crisp white shirt open at the throat. It would be a warm day, of course, and no one wore neckties much anyway during the summer, but when he entered the store he seemed to have just stepped out of a laundry box in his casual, fresh attire.

Frank was busy with a customer in the hardware section. If he saw his father he didn't let on. John made a mental note to have a talk with Frank. He didn't want the difference between the elders to trickle down to the youngsters.

Levinsky was to the point. He nodded once, which was his only concession to convention, then he said, " I've got an order. My office phoned up yesterday to say a highway construction job I bid down upstate was awarded, and I got it."

John stiffened. He had no intention of doing a cent's worth of business with Meyer Levinsky under the circumstances. That would be all he'd need—for the natives to learn Levinsky had placed a large order with the emporium.

Levinsky fished out a thick sheaf of typed pages. " Ordinarily I'd do business through my wholesale houses in New York," he said, smoothing out the papers and not looking at John. " But this job happens to be only forty miles from Newport, and three hundred miles from the city. Common sense says transportation costs on the steel and stuff will be a hell of a lot less from here." He raised his eyes, read John's expression and straightened up off the counter. " Look, Leavitt; it's got nothing at all to do with that damned piece of ground." He made a disparaging little gesture. " All right; when I first came in here last year I suggested I might be able to throw some business your way if things worked out on the discothéque. Frankly, I didn't like myself when I said that. But, in case you don't know, that's how business is done in the big cities. You scratch my back, I scratch yours." Leavitt thumped the papers. " This is different. It's an order. It's nothing but straight business."

" Tell the town that, Mister Levinsky, and they'd laugh in your face. I'm sorry." John dropped his gaze to the specification sheets on the counter. " It would have been a nice order."

Levinsky's face screwed up. " Would have been . . .? Leavitt; I can guess your mark-up. You'd make damned near a year's full profit off this one order!"

John was candid. " More than a year's profit; you've got an exaggerated notion of my net, Mister Levinsky."

" And—you won't do it?"

" No."

Levinsky groaned and leaned on the counter. He turned to gaze over to where his son was talking with a rough-looking man about one of the new line of outboard motors. He saw Miss Emily through the glass partition of the office. He said, " Leavitt—I'm going to give the city that goddamned cemetery. You guys can have it for free. Look; forget I ever wanted to do anything in this town." The tough, troubled eyes swung round. " I'm sorry as hell I wasn't born with a name like Winthrop or Morgan or Hudson or Adams—or Leavitt. You want to know something; sometimes it gets kind of hard to breathe in Newport. You ever had that sensation? No, you never have." Levinsky reached for the papers on the counter.

John waited until the spasm was past then he said, " Keep it, Mister Levinsky. Don't give it to the town."

Levinsky went right ahead folding the sheaf of papers.

" If you think giving the town back their cemetery will make it any easier, you're wrong. I'm no flaming liberal, Mister Levinsky, but I'm not a dug-in conservative either. You made a fair offer. The town didn't like it. At least *part* of the town didn't. So now you tuck your tail. You get disgusted and throw it all up. Mister Levinsky, you're doing the one thing no New Englander will ever forgive you for. You're quitting before the fight has even begun."

Levinsky shook his head. "Leavitt; I've been fighting all my lousy life. I've gotten rich fighting and winning. But this ain't it; we came here and made our second home to have peace, not war."

"You bought a war, Levinsky, when you bought that cemetery at the tax-sale. You don't have any choice. Unless of course you don't give a damn about your self-respect or the respect of the people around Newport. No one cares now that you came here for peace. All they care about now is: What kind of man is this—Jew—Meyer Levinsky?"

The two men stood looking steadily at one another for a moment. Meyer Levinsky then said very quietly, "Damn; I didn't know one of you cold codfish could get fired up. Okay, Leavitt. But I'll tell you something—you've been a traitor today. If your native-friends heard what you just said to me they'd tar and feather you. You just talked them into a fight with Meyer Levinsky—who knows how to fight, believe me!"

John smiled. "Excuse me, my book-keeper is signalling I'm wanted on the telephone."

"Yeah," said Meyer Levinsky and walked out of the store.

It was Jeremy Benson on the phone. He wanted to report that he'd " run the books ", as you called it, at the law library over at the court-house, and what he'd thought might be the case respecting permission to remove the old graves was essentially correct, although by law the town would be obliged also to run a series of notices in the newspapers announcing intent and inviting comment from descendants.

" Otherwise," Jeremy said, " it's pretty much as I thought. But that's not what I called you about. I did some checking on this Levinsky chap. He's a very rich man, John, and his reputation in the city is good. Tough but good. His word is his bond, and in a place like New York City that's very rare. So . . ." Benson took in a big breath and let it out. ". . . So, I had to turn Ed down a little while ago when he came to my office with several others to engage me to represent the town in a suit of recovery against Levinsky."

John was shocked. " Suit of recovery? You mean on the tax-redemption angle, Jeremy?"

" Yes."

" Well hell, Jeremy, the town treasury is broke. How the hell can we—anyway—Ed had no right to do that on his own. All three of us have to concur before anything like that can be undertaken. Moreover, Jeremy; who's going to pay you?"

Benson laughed a harsh little snorting laugh. " Who ever worries about who's going to pay an attorney, John? I told Ed I couldn't represent him as an individual since I'm already on annual retainer for the town. I also told him essentially what you just said—he had no right to come up here breathing fire without the approval of you and Charley as Selectmen. And finally, I told him if he was smart he'd stick to his damned plumbing business." Jeremy was momentarily silent, then said, in a less harsh tone, " I can't imagine what's got into Ed. He's usually Charley's boy all right, but he never takes the initiative like he's doing this time."

" Charley," said John. " Charley's behind it somehow. He came round to see me talking compromise. Said the bank had lost a few accounts."

" That happens to be true. I'm one of the directors so I know it's true. Also; the directors chewed Charley out for making such a big issue—*personal* issue—of the old cemetery. He didn't like it one bit. Sometimes Charley's a mite big for his britches. But then you know Charley."

" Yes indeed," said John. " It's Ed I'm having trouble understanding."

Benson was bland. " Don't worry about him. As a plumber Ed's pretty good, but if he starts pretending he's something bigger I'll personally turn one of his faucets off on him."

Afterwards, thinking it all over in the seclusion of the office, John had to smile at Jeremy's last remark. But of course that had been facetious, and palpably Ed wasn't being the least bit funny.

He considered calling Charley but didn't do it.

Frank came in with another boat-motor contract to be approved. This time John didn't even look at the purchaser's signature. He said, " Is he good for it, Frank?" The lanky youth nodded and John then said, " Fine. And Frank. After this make the approvals yourself." He smiled. " If you lose one I'll take it out of your pay." Frank was almost to the door when John spoke again. " Come in here at quitting time, Frank. I'd like a word with you."

Miss Emily looked up, watched Frank leave, turned and said, " Why isn't the father more like the boy?"

John had an answer for that. " Why aren't you more like your mother? Because you came up a lot easier than she did, Miss Emily. Why am I not more taciturn and grim like my father? Because I've never come within a long breath of losing everything in a Depression. Meyer Levinsky's tough and brash and ungrammatical, but he's honest, Miss Emily. You don't have to like his type but you've got to respect the ability and the strength—and the honesty."

Miss Emily looked long at John then quietly went back to work. It was approaching statement-time. She'd have plenty to do without getting too involved in other things.

At quitting time Frank came into the office drying his hands on a soiled handkerchief. He'd evidently washed in a hurry neglecting to look in the mirror because he had a smudge of grease on his forehead.

" Yes, sir?" he said, stopping half-way to John's desk. John held up a clean cup. " Coffee?"

" No, thank you. Never cared much for it."

" Frank; about the cemetery . . ."

" Mister Leavitt; in the store I'm a clerk with merchandise to handle and sell. Nothing else comes up. I've said that fifty times in the past few days to customers. I say it now to you also. I told the customers they didn't even have to like me if they didn't want to; I'm selling good merchandise and I'll make it good on my word if they aren't satisfied once they get it home. I'll service their things and I'll get up special orders for things we don't carry that they want. But in the store I'm a clerk—a salesman—nothing else."

Miss Emily was watching the youth, a pencil poised. Her vinegary old eyes swivelled to John, who was filling a cup with coffee. John turned and said, " Quite a speech, son, but I only wanted to ask one question, not try to be very logical. I just wanted to say if any of this is painful for you, or disagreeable, or complicated at home—tell me."

Frank finished wiping his hands, stowed the limp handkerchief, flung back his wavy hair and looked straight at John. "I've felt more popular a time or two in my life," he said dryly, "but I can live with it very well, Mister Leavitt. Jerrie says my father is right."

"And you, Frank, what do you say?"

"Well; I told Jerrie it's not my father who is really involved and likely to get hurt, it's you. I told her I asked my father to give back the damned—excuse me Miss Emily—cemetery; that we're outsiders and what he's trying to do here might be fine in the city, but not up here."

"Well, son, he tried to give back the cemetery this morning and I told him he was a quitter."

Both Frank and Miss Emily looked shocked. John strolled to the desk, sat on the corner of it and sipped his black coffee. He smiled. "I also told him New Englanders don't like cowards; that he'd bought a battle with that piece of ground, and unless he wanted to confirm in a lot of biased New England minds that—Jews—are yellow, he'd better make a damned good fight of it."

Miss Emily's jaw sagged. She stared straight at her employer. Frank didn't move a muscle until John smiled. Then he said, "Oh Lord. That's all my father will need, Mister Leavitt," and groaned. "I've got to get home if you don't need me any more."

John waved towards the door. "Good night, Frank."

For a full thirty seconds after the boy had departed

Miss Emily fumbled with her hat and coat. She didn't get the hat on straight even then, which was understandable perhaps since a mirror had never been allowed in the office, it sat atop her head like a year-old bird nest. She said, " Mister Leavitt; you sounded just like a— Democrat."

John set aside the empty cup. " Miss Emily; of all the folks in this town there aren't very many whose opinion I care a damn for, but you happen to be one of them. Just tell me this: Am I right or am I wrong?"

" It depends on what you're talking about, Mister Leavitt."

" You know damned well what I'm talking about!"

Miss Emily sniffed. " Seems to me," she said sharply, " you've been using an awful lot of profanity lately. All right, I'll tell you—you're right. But don't you expect a Trotten—a *fourth generation* Trotten—ever to admit that in public. And now good night sir!"

John held the door for her. The store was quiet, the lights had been turned low. He was alone in the place for the first time in many months. He looked around, waggled his head and went after his own coat and hat.

Sounded just like a—*Democrat*!

In solidly Republican New England that was like saying he'd sounded like a—well an illegitimate.

CHAPTER FOURTEEN

Charley Hudson Revealed

CHARLEY CAME by the store with his usual disagreeable expression, only deeper this day as he barged into the office, threw Miss Emily a short, curt nod—they were related—and said, " John; we've got a real problem. I had a county appraiser over, from the Assessor's office, and he put the value of the old cemetery at twenty thousand dollars. I also happen to know Levinsky paid one thousand dollars for it. Now, as I see it, the town can sue and—"

" Charley," said John dryly, " you already know every answer to all the statements you're going to make in my office today because you sent Ed to see Jeremy Benson— and I talked to Jeremy afterwards. Now let's cut out all the beating round the damned bush: Just what exactly did you come in here to tell me today?"

The banker glowered at John's tone as well as at his bluntness. He swivelled one swift look at Miss Emily and that would normally have been her cue to remember something elsewhere and leave the office, but she sat on as oblivious to Hudson's presence as though he weren't in the same room with her.

" I'm trying to keep this reasonable," said Charley. " I say we've got a good cause for legal action."

" Jeremy doesn't think so."

" We can still redeem that piece of land. There's a year of grace to do it in."

" Then what's the hurry, Charley? Let's wait and see what develops."

Hudson's neck reddened. " John; at the meeting you wanted immediate action. Now you want delay. What the devil *do* you want?"

John went to the percolator. " Coffee, Charley?"

" No!"

" I'll tell you what I want. For one thing I'm curious about Ed—why did he make that fake trip to see Jeremy with some friends as though he were about to organise the community for action? Ed's a follower, Charley, never a leader. Secondly; what are you trying to do—talking compromise one minute, fight the next?"

Hudson's anger was near the boiling point. He waited a moment as though to control it, then he said, " John; you're not trying to help one damned bit, and while I didn't come down here to mention this maybe I ought to tell you anyway—there's a re-call movement afoot to have you removed as a Selectman."

Miss Emily's eyes got round. Even John, pouring himself a cup of coffee, was surprised. But he finished pouring and returned to his desk before he said, " Fair enough, Charley; that's the prerogative of the folks who voted me into office." He didn't sit down behind the desk but looked Charley straight in the eye. " But if this is another underhanded trick of yours, believe me you'll regret it."

Charley's anger nearly tore loose at that remark, but

he managed to get to the door before he spoke. "Underhanded trick, eh? By God, John, you're pushing pretty hard for a fight with the bank."

He slammed out of the office.

Miss Emily almost said something but the look on John's face changed her mind. She ducked her head and went back to work.

John had his coffee and afterwards went out into the store. There were a number of customers, including Caleb Adams, who was talking to Frank over near the display of outboard motors. John got busy waiting on customers. He worked off his indignation against Charley in that manner and afterwards when they had a breather Frank came over to say he was sorry he'd wasted so much time with Caleb but he couldn't get away.

"He was all fired up on the cemetery issue, Mister Leavitt. I tried to get a word in edgeways to explain we only talked shop during working hours round here and never got it said."

John grinned. "Frank; one thing you'll have to learn is that this store has been the community spit-and-whittle-club around Newport for a hundred years. Especially during the winter, the folks who stand around aren't going to buy, they've just come to exchange views and hear the latest gossip."

"That won't help the daily receipts any," said Frank.

"No. But we can't get into every pocket that comes in, Frank, and we can't very well change community habit either, when it's so deeply entrenched. I'm not even sure we ought to change it. There's enough change coming as it is. The emporium is sort of a last refuge for the older generations."

Frank had to depart to care for a customer and John stood thoughtfully watching him, remembering in his own youth how energetic he'd also been.

Later, he called Jeremy and got a surprise. The attorney said he'd been approached by a building syndicate concerning the title on the old cemetery. " They wanted to know whether the town intended to sue for redemption, John, and all I could tell them was that such a course was up to the Selectmen."

" What was their interest?"

" Well now, John, you didn't descend in the last rain; they wanted to get hold of the property and put a building on it to rent to local storekeepers and professional people."

John felt like he'd just been kicked in the stomach when a disconcerting thought struck hard. " Charley . . .?"

" Of course, Charley. They didn't say so. They didn't even mention his name. But they *did* mention Ed, so for the hell of it I pulled an old trick. I called Ed on the phone, said I was Staiger, one of the men who came to see me, and said old Benson wasn't very co-operative."

" And . . .?"

" And Ed told me to go see Charley at the bank; that he'd know whatever had to be done next."

John rang off, sat down behind his desk and slowly let it all drop into place. The offer to compromise hadn't been deceit after all, it had been Charley's way of trying to smooth things out so that getting title to the land might be accomplished through the orderly processes, in order that he and his silent-partners might then get hold of the land. The latest visit to the store by the banker had been to insinuate a threat unless John co-operated. But that hadn't come off any better than the offer to compromise had.

Charley would now have to come up with something else. Even his attempt at organising a group of citizens, with Ed as spokesman, hadn't jelled. Old Benson had spiked that at the outset. But John knew Charley Hudson, had known him all his life, and whatever else Charley Hudson was, a quitter was not among his virtues or vices.

He went home to find Madge and Jerrie preparing for a cook-out in the backyard. Frank would be over later, his daughter told him, but when Frank showed up he also had Uncle Caleb with him. He explained to the others while Caleb was in the kitchen getting a drink of water, that when he went out to his car the old man was sitting in it and short of bodily ejecting old Caleb, he couldn't get rid of him.

John laughed. So did Madge. They knew most of Caleb's idiosyncrasies and this was a common enough one. When he decided to go visiting he wasn't to be put off by so slight an oversight as the lack of an invitation. Madge went after another steak while Jerrie set another place at the redwood barbecue table.

Caleb had on a clean shirt—un-ironed but freshly washed—and he made a poor attempt at shaving as well. He seemed more frail to John and Madge, when she brought out the lemonade, gave Caleb a special glass—it had less lemon and more sugar. But the old man's mind was as sharp as ever. When he and John were sitting back in shade he said, " Son; had some visitors today. City-men from the looks of 'em. Mentioned Charley Hudson's name."

John was blank. He could guess who the city-men

were but he couldn't guess their purpose in going down to see Caleb Adams.

"They wanted to buy my land, John."

That neatly cleared up the mystery. "Did they say Charley sent them?"

"Not exactly, but you know how folks do sometimes—talk down to an old geezer like maybe he doesn't have all his wits. They wanted to sub-divide the land, sell off lots to summer folks, and make a marina out where my old dock is. They offered a crazy price for the land."

"You agreed?"

Cal snorted and shot John a withering look. "You know a cussed sight better'n that. How many times have folks wanted to buy the homestead in the past twenty years? I never kept track but I'd say at least a hundred times. I always give them the same answer. Not interested. Been living here too many years to change habits now. Fight over it after I'm gone."

John was interested in the men. "Was one of them named Staiger, Cal?"

"Didn't pay that much attention, son. Three of 'em. Neckties, little narrow-brim hats, low shoes and a nice automobile. Do you know them too?"

John shook his head about the time Madge brought over their plates and made Caleb edge up closer to the table, which he did obediently enough, but when Madge walked off he grumbled something about not being a little child, consarn it.

Frank and Jerrie didn't have much to say during the meal. They were politely attentive but quiet. Madge had to carry most of the conversation with Caleb helping out between mouthfuls, but since he wasn't too well equipped in the fang department he had to concentrate most of the time on just chewing.

John, busy with some private thoughts, arose to help with the talk now and then, but until his wife looked exasperatedly at him he kept returning to other things. Finally though, when Madge and Jerrie went after the ice-cream dessert, he came to the party. After that the conversation became lively enough. By the time Frank and Jerrie excused themselves and left, taking Frank's car as they headed for the river, Caleb had made everyone laugh with anecdotes concerning people he'd known —most of whom had been dead some years, but whom Madge and her husband had known.

It was a successful party even after the youngsters had gone, and old Caleb, with a decent woman-cooked meal under his belt for the first time in ages, scintillated. He also drank more of the weakened but sweetened lemonade.

It was typical of the old man that he never watched the time nor gave a thought to how he'd get home. In former years he'd made the long walk without a thought, and typically now, his mind still operated that way. But he was no longer a spry sixty. Frank had been solicitous to John out of the old man's hearing, but John had said for Frank and Jerrie to go on, he'd take old Caleb home.

On the drive through the warm mid-summer night John made a suggestion that perhaps Caleb ought to sell out and get a cottage closer to town. The old man doggedly shook his head. "I was born there and I'll die there, son."

John said no more about it although he began for the first time in his life to worry about the oncoming winter.

Clearly, Caleb was no longer able to cope with eighteen inches of snow, or the bitter, deadly cold that accompanied it. He made up his mind something would have to be done about old Caleb before winter came.

There was a smoky old moon riding across a star-lighted sky when they pulled in down beside Caleb's old home. Seen through the lattice of ancient tree-climbs it was enormous in size and close in distance. Down where the rotting old sagging boat-landing stood, river water lapped softly, and farther out, mid-way in the river, a sailboat lay at anchor, sails furled, riding lights winking red and green.

Caleb stood on the weathered porch looking round. "No one hangs on forever," he mused, watching that graceful boat far out. " Of course when a feller's young he's sure that out of all the millions of folks, he's the only one that's immortal. But when he gets to pushing eighty, well, he commences to have his doubts, John . . .?"

" Yes, Cal?"

" Well; it's a little embarrassing to say this, but the time is close, I think, so I'd better tell someone." Caleb stood stooped and frail in the soft moonlight looking away from John. " I used to want to be buried beside my folks, but I got a fresh idea now. Thought about it quite a bit lately. Thought maybe a man can help out a little dead, same as alive." The old man looked sharply at John. " I still want to be buried beside my folks, son, but now I want us all buried in one of those new graveyards."

" New ones?"

" Don't look so damned surprised, John, you know blessed well the old one's going to get moved soon. Well; whichever one Levinsky offers and you fellers accept, I want to be buried in it beside my folks. Will you look after that for me?"

" Yes, I'll look after it for you."

" Well; that's really what I came up to see you about tonight, only at a party it's just not seemly talking about things like that. So I figured you'd take me home and we'd get it talked over. Good night, John."

" Good night, Caleb."

John drove half-way home with a blurred twinkle in his eye and a soft little lump in his throat. Caleb's body might be wearing out but his mind surely wasn't.

CHAPTER FIFTEEN

Revelation by Moonlight

MADGE HAD a picnic-supper packed and ready the next evening when John arrived home. It was very warm out, and it had been a scorching day with people complaining all over town, even in the emporium where inordinately high ceilings and a big overhead fan didn't do much more than soften the blow of the physical heat. It'd been a sluggish and lethargic day.

Madge told John to put his bathing suit on under his shirt and trousers, that they'd cool off in the river. He was limp enough to appreciate the idea, but he smiled and said, " Moonlight swimming, at our age?"

Madge had evidently expected that. She said, " I can remember when you'd have been the first one in."

They went alone because, as Madge said, Jerrie'd had a date. She and Frank with several other couples were having a party somewhere down along the river tonight. She also said, sounding sombre, " John; I'm afraid it's serious and I don't know what to do about it."

He'd given the same dilemma some thought lately although he'd purposely neglected mentioning it to Madge. " She's almost twenty," he said, driving through the silver-soft and pulsing-warm night. " What can anyone do about things that involve twenty-year-old daughters, Madge? Keep good thoughts and hope for the best."

" But . . ."

" Yes. But what?"

" Well, I realise she's been to college and all, and is sophisticated for a small-town girl, but I wonder if Frank is right for her?"

He said gently, " And if he isn't right for her, Madge, could you convince her of that if she's in love with him?"

They reached the beach and turned off to drive through a tangle of trees and seagrapes and scrub brush until they were on Caleb's land, then John followed a well-worn set of ancient ruts to a patch of empty, white-sand beach. They had to leave the car back in some trees where the earth was hard, otherwise they'd have got it stuck in sand. The walk was only a hundred or so yards so John carried the wicker hamper while Madge brought along their towels and pillows.

It was the kind of thing they'd loved to do back during their high-school, college and dating days. What heightened the effect that nothing had changed was the same moon, the same river and beach and a hot mid-summer night. There really was nothing very different as long as they stayed on Caleb's long stretch of river frontage, but elsewhere, hidden now by soft darkness, everything else was changed.

She had fried chicken and had made potato salad with scallions, things she'd made years back and of which he was very fond. Later, stripped to bathing suits, he privately thought that she did not look much different two decades later. It had always surprised—and pleased—him, that she'd been able to retain so much of that youthful beauty. Other people they'd known all their lives seemed to have changed considerably, the men bald, fat, pasty, the women thick, sluggish, overly made up with cosmetics.

He looked and sighed softly and felt content, so he said, "Madge; I'm not so sure Frank's wrong for her. I concede the differences. I also concede that in our day it wouldn't have come this close, in all probability, but this is another time, another era."

"Is he good at the store?" she wanted to know.

"Best man I ever had."

"You're biased, John. What does Miss Emily think?"

"Ask her yourself. She said he's the best one of the lot we've had working for us."

Madge smiled softly, looking out over the water. "I don't suppose anyone could top that, could they? Emily's a down-east Yankee if ever there was one. She wouldn't compliment a person unless she had to."

"He's an odd boy in some ways," John mused. "He's good in the store but I sometimes wonder if he doesn't work so hard with the customers because he's more interested in their responses, their thought-processes, than in selling merchandise. Not that he doesn't sell. He's better than I am at that. But he seems sometimes to be looking more closely at the individuals as *people*—or maybe I should have said he looks more closely at the people as *individuals*—than as customers." John smiled at her. "I'm not expressing this very well. Anyway, it's just an idea; I haven't really thought much about it."

She looked back at the water. "Wait and see, I keep telling myself. I also keep telling myself that at least we should be grateful Frank likes Newport and won't take her down to the city to live. Then too, they seemed to like the same things." She looked back. "But a mother has a struggle, John. A secret struggle day and night when this time approaches."

He was quietly affirmative about that. "Don't exclude fathers, love. I don't suppose there was ever a father who thought any boy alive was good enough for his little daughter." He shifted position. "Have we waited long enough after eating to go in now?"

She arose with the moon on her far side, ran a hand under her loose, curly hair and he caught his breath. She looked exactly in every line and detail as she'd looked twenty-five years before. It was incredible.

She saw his expression, slowly smiled and said, "Well . . .?"

He reached but she evaded him easily. "For a man

who might be a grandfather in a couple of years you're not acting the part tonight."

They went down and dived in. The water was warm close to the shore but colder farther out. The exercise made him feel more youthful than he'd felt in a long while. She had always been a better swimmer than he was, but she'd also never made a point of it. Madge was a remarkable woman exactly as she'd also been a remarkable girl.

They reached Caleb's old landing and clung to the pilings for a rest. A patched, warped and weathered boat was tied loosely near by. As he looked at the forlorn old craft he recalled what Caleb had said to him the night before, and told her all of it. They then swam back towards their beach and stood a while in the shallow water savouring the blessed coolness of hot air on wet skin.

She'd brought some beer along, which she detested but which he occasionally liked and drank. They went after that. She had a Coca-Cola kneeling in the sand with her curly hair a frightful mess, her wet smooth face soft-lighted and youthful, and smiling as he looked at her, knowing intuitively what his thoughts were.

They thought they were quite alone until down the beach in the middle distance a fire suddenly flickered to life and youthful voices rose in quick sentences.

The fire rose, spitting sparks, twisting, turning, reddening then paling as it took hard hold of whatever kind of old wood was feeding it. The people down there, all young, were too lively to be anything but young, and John, sipping his beer, thought he heard a familiar voice.

Everyone fled the fire leaving one couple beside it,

evidently cooks while the others screeched and sprang into the water. For a while the diminishing howls of swimmers lingered, then grew soft as some sort of aquatic race developed in the warm river.

The couple tending the fire evidently finished laying out the food and setting weiners to boil in a pan atop some rocks beside the fire, because they arose and started slowly pacing down the beach beyond Caleb's old boat-landing. They were silhouetted by the moon, by gentle reflection off the river, by their own lightness as they came past the landing towards the stretch of beach where Madge and John sat.

John knew the girl while the hand-in-hand couple were still a long way off. He was sure he also knew the boy. The beer in his hand was forgotten. At his side, Madge was like stone. She'd also recognised the girl, evidently.

Then the couple stopped almost as though by pre-arrangement. They didn't see John and Madge. Even if they'd been looking round, which neither of them were, they'd still have had to strain to make out anything that far off, but because they were both standing, John and Madge saw them clearly; even heard the boy say, " I did all that thinking you said to do, Jerrie."

She reached up to touch his face. She was profiled to her parents. She was physically very like her mother. It showed, especially in a bathing suit.

" You were right, of course. So was Uncle Caleb. Honey; we can't make a mistake in this."

" And . . . ?" the girl said, her one word riding as clear as a struck chord in the endless night.

" I want to marry you, Jerrie. I know it's right."

She raised her other arm. They blended in the moonlight and John's grip on the beer can left a deep indentation.

They parted. She said, "What will your folks say, Frank?"

His answer was another question. "What will *yours* say? I'm not worried about my folks at all. You know my mother adores you. And my dad—well—you know how he is; it's never been easy for him to show affection; it embarrasses him."

"I've done a foolish thing," said Jerrie. "I've kept—us—to myself around home. I can't explain exactly why and I've never done that before. My parents are wonderful people."

"Yes," he agreed, taking her hands and holding her a foot or two away. "Your mother's as pretty as you are. Your dad's tops. He's a combination of old and new. The only thing I worry about—is how they'll get along."

"You're thinking of the cemetery?"

Frank's voice turned cutting-sharp, almost fierce. "I wish dad'd never seen that damned thing. I wish he'd just deed it over to the town or give it to someone—or forget he ever bought it."

She pulled at him, yanking him to her. They blended again, he bending down slightly, she standing on tiptoe.

John looked at Madge then at the beer can in his hand with the deep dent in it. Madge looked away from the couple locked together up the beach with the moon behind them, too.

John blew his breath out softly.

Jerrie and Frank turned back, hand-in-hand, towards the popping blaze, their progress slow, their heads bent in quiet conversation.

E

What little beer was in the can tasted flat so John poured it out upon the sand. In a second it had disappeared. He put the empty can back into their hamper and Madge, taking her cue from that, began putting away their dishes and utensils. Neither of them spoke for a long while.

The faint cry of effervescent youth far up the beach rang softly in the quiet where the other youngsters were straggling back after their race in the water. Someone, either Frank or Jerrie, pitched more wood into the fire; it blazed and crackled.

John said, " I don't like the feeling of being an eavesdropping parent, do you?"

Madge shook her head face averted as she packed their things away to hide the bright wetness of her eyes.

" No. But perhaps it's better to get the shock like this than to wait in knowing agony for them to come round and tell you when you're not expecting it."

He helped her gather the towels, the pillows, their beach blanket. She was right, of course, but he still felt mean about what he'd seen and heard. As they arose to go back he said, " Honey; it was going to happen someday."

She dumbly nodded and started walking ahead of him.

He didn't say any more until they'd backed the car out, turned and were heading back. Even then all he said was, " Next time we'd better build a fire of our own." What he meant, of course, was so that they'd have their own blazing signal to let others know they were out there, too.

There were lights showing in Caleb's house, which meant he was up, probably listening to the radio or reading. He had, of course, known the youngsters were down there on his beach; they were down there, it seemed, almost every night.

" John? What about the Levinskys?"

He knew exactly what she meant although the question itself gave him no clue, but a man doesn't live with a woman more than twenty years without sensing things that lie unspoken in her mind.

" Well; I suppose we just wait, love. I suppose they just wait too. After all, we all belong to another generation; this isn't our affair, really, no matter how much we want to believe it is. Jerrie'll come to us soon now. I'm sure of that. And like you said back there—at least we'll not be caught flat-footed."

Madge held her robe close in front, laid her wet curls upon his shoulder and silently cried all the way home. The ancient moon continued its soaring ride, having witnessed nothing anywhere on earth, least of all on old Caleb's beach, it hadn't witnessed millions of times before, and otherwise the world wasn't changed anywhere, except perhaps in the poignant hearts of a mother and a father— unless, of course, it was also changed in the younger hearts of two lovers back there by their crackling beach-fire.

CHAPTER SIXTEEN

Out in the Open

JOHN EYED Frank all the following day in a new light. He was a calm, quiet, thoughtful man most of the time and his thought-processes, formed years ago, were eminently orderly and visionary. By mid-day he'd already decided Frank would make an ideal successor for him when the time came. He was even grateful for that because, having had only one child, a daughter, he had occasionally reflected upon the future of the historic old family store when he got too old to operate it.

Of course there was this business of Frank wanting to be a writer, but he shrugged that off much as Frank's father had done; it wasn't a very practical idea. At least in the eyes of a third-generation storekeeper like John Leavitt it wasn't.

When he returned from having lunch with Madge, Miss Emily said Charley Hudson had called to remind John there'd be a Selectmen's meeting the following night. That annoyed him. He'd never missed a single meeting, had never even been tardy. Why should Charley have to remind him this time?

Then he had a hunch and called Jeremy Benson. The attorney was laconically wry. " No one's started suit yet, John, but I had it on good authority over at the county seat that Ed Smith's been over there with three strangers poring over the old tax-rolls and boning up on all the redemption procedures. I'll tell you what I think, John; I think Ed and Charley are about to drop some kind of bomb in our midst."

John was inclined to agree, and he also thought he knew when it would be dropped—the very next night at the Selectmen's meeting—the particular meeting Charley wanted to be sure John would attend.

That evening after closing time he drove out to Ed's plumbing works on the north end of town and caught Ed at his desk. The look on the plumber's face when John walked in and nodded was part astonishment, part guilt, but he rallied swiftly and boomed out a hearty greeting, then got John a chair before retiring behind his littered desk again to say, " Odd thing happened today, John; you remember that school job I won the bid on?"

John nodded; he had reason to remember it since Ed had walked out without letting John order any of the essential parts for him.

" Well; today some government inspectors came in and told me they wanted to see my list of materials. Said they were watching what went into all new schools closely these days. And damned if they didn't turn thumbs down on about half the stuff I figured to install." Ed leaned back and waved a hand over the pile of papers and catalogues atop his desk. " That's what I was doing when you came in; trying to figure costs on the alternative stuff they said I'd have to substitute. And it doesn't look very good cost-wise so far."

John said, " That's too bad, Ed. But you're an old hand. You'll come out all right."

" Sure I will, only I don't understand; I've never had this happen before. It's almost like they'd singled me out."

John got a jolting thought, sat and studied Ed's face a moment, then put the thought aside and said, " Ed; don't let Charley use you."

The plumber instantly grew wary. " What are you talkin' about?"

" The cemetery. And you damned well know what I'm talking about. Don't let him get you sucked into some scheme he may be hatching. Now Ed," John held up a hand in the face of a certain explosion, " just wait a minute before you sound off. I'm not going to lecture you. I'm not even going to tell you about the things you've been up to, for Charley, with Mister Staiger and those other city-men. All I'm going to say is—tomorrow night at the meeting be careful, Ed, very careful. You're an elected town official. Don't let Charley suck you into acting in any other capacity."

Ed's face turned ferret-like and wise. He said, " I guess someone ought to tell you, John, it's *you* that's acting against Newport's best interests, wanting to see Levinsky keep the cemetery and build his coffee-house. And there's been a lot of talk."

" Re-call petition," murmured John, arising. " Ed; I'll resign the minute you start pushing it. But I'll promise you something else. The minute I resign and can attend the meetings as a private citizen, I'm going to throw everything I know straight at you and Charley in front of the whole damned town."

" Huh! *What* do you know, John? Just give me one example!"

" Just one? All right. You and Charley's city-friends

over at the courthouse today trying to figure some way to beat Levinsky's title to that land. That's just one. Nice talking to you, Ed. Good night."

On the drive home John had to smile in recollection of the crumpled look on Ed's face as he'd left the shop. Ed wasn't a leader, but on the other hand he wasn't so dumb he didn't know at once how that would have sounded if there'd been other people in his office at the time John had spoken of Ed's slyness at the courthouse, either. Ed would do a lot of thinking before tomorrow night. Of course he'd also go running straight to Charley. But that was all right.

Madge looked enquiringly at him when he came into the kitchen. Jerrie was there making a tossed salad and threw him a kiss. Madge said he was a half-hour late and he made a joke of it without mentioning where he'd been. He also made a joke of the fact that Jerrie was home for a change and she shot him in a rueful little grin.

After supper Jerrie went out back up under the big tree with them and that, obviously, portended something which John knew in his heart was going to be serious because he also knew what it was.

Madge made it easy. " Jerrie; your father told me that Miss Emily said Frank was the best bo—man—they'd had working at the store."

Jerrie fidgeted on the chair. Madge had given her the opening and now she hesitated. Madge went farther. " He's very nice, too."

" Mother," Jerrie said sudden-swift. " Dad, I'm in love with Frank."

That evoked no visible astonishment from either of

her parents. They didn't gasp nor throw up their hands nor even blink their eyes. But neither did they utter a sound.

" We— Actually, I've been seeing a lot of him and I'm ashamed that I didn't tell you."

John was dry about that. " Honey, it hasn't exactly been a secret."

" Well; I know, Dad, but—it's serious."

Madge smiled and touched her daughter's wrist with light, soft fingers. " It's always serious," she murmured.

" I want to marry him," said Jerrie, her eyes dark and wondering as she looked from one parent to the other. " He asked me, last night."

The silence ran on a bit longer after that statement than John thought was necessary, so to ease the strain he said, " Would you object to a couple of questions, honey?"

" No."

" Well; the first one is—do you plan to stay in Newport?"

" I want to. So does Frank."

John nodded, his mouth curling into a little gentle smile. " And the other question is: Do the Levinskys know?"

" Frank was to tell them this evening. We're going to meet later. He'll be by for me."

" Then," said John, " your mother and I wish you all the success in the world, honey."

The three of them sat in awkward silence a moment before Madge sprang up saying she'd get them all a tiny highball because people drank a toast on occasions like this, and fled for the house. John watched her go, knowing that tears were blinding her. To avert Jerrie's attention and give his wife the precious moment alone every mother needed at this very special time in her life, he said, " I was wondering, Jerrie: Will Frank keep on working at the store?"

" We—haven't talked much about that, really. I think so. But he wants to finish his book."

" Oh. The book. Yes. By the way, what's he call it?"

" *To face the sun.*"

John deliberated on that. It seemed an arty enough title for a book; at least it seemed in line with some of the book titles he'd seen on the book-racks at the drugstore where most books were sold in Newport.

" It has a nice sound," he conceded. " What's the story about?"

" Newport, Daddy. Newport, only with a different name, and the people in it. How they think and react and do things. It's really surprisingly good." Jerrie blushed. " I didn't mean it shouldn't be a good story."

He laughed. " I know what you meant, Jerrie. I've never known an author before. I'll expect an autographed copy when it comes out."

She broke, finally, threw herself into his arms like she'd done innumerable times before when she'd been a child and life had overpowered her, or problems had been too big for her. He swallowed the hard lump in his throat. " My gosh, Jerrie, you're twenty years old."

With her face pushed flat against his shoulder she said, " Not right this minute I'm not."

She recovered by the time Madge came up, smiling, with their weak Tom Collinses. Madge had recovered too; in fact if he hadn't been married to her for so long

E*

he'd never have been able to tell she'd had her cry, washed her face in cold water and put fresh make-up on.

"Here's to Jerrie and Frank—and lots of—"

Madge hurriedly broke in. "Happiness, dear Jerrie. No matter what else ever comes—happiness. It's better than money any day."

They drank and talked and finished the highballs when Jerrie detected a sound John missed entirely; Frank's car swishing to the kerbing out front. She gave them both a quick, smeary kiss and bolted, leaving an empty glass and a chair.

Madge looked up. "Would you like another one," she asked her husband, "and stronger this time?"

He handed her the glass, watched her go towards the house again, then put both hands behind his head and thought of a lot of things back down a kaleidoscope of years to the second year of their married life when Jerrie had first arrived. Then, by repeating the process in reverse he watched her grow up again in his mind's eye.

The second drink was considerably stronger. In fact he wondered if perhaps Madge hadn't been short of mix and had made up for it with the gin.

But its effect was pleasant. He felt wonderfully sluggish —and sad.

Madge said she hadn't expected Jerrie to come to them the very next night, but he was philosophical about that. After what they'd inadvertently seen last night, he said, it wouldn't have been too good for them to have postponed doing something about marriage.

Madge shot him a quick look, partly disapproving. He shrugged. "Chemistry, love. Purest chemistry. We were that age too, once, and I still remember it very vividly."

Madge blushed, then smiled and changed the subject. " I wonder how Frank made out. You know Mister Levinsky better than I, John. How would he react?"

It was difficult to imagine. John knew Meyer Levinsky the businessman. Not Meyer Levinsky the parent. The only genuine clue he had was what he'd overheard Frank say on the beach the night before. Basing his assumption on that he risked a guess.

" Blustery, I suppose. Practical. ' How will you live, son?' sort of thing. But no objections. I don't really know Mrs. Levinsky at all; have only seen her a dozen times at most, and I suppose in an affair of this kind the mothers figure more prominently."

Madge swished her glass until the ice made soft music in the glass. " I'll wait a day or two then go visit her," she said, sounding very matter-of-fact about this proposal. " There is one thing that occurs to me, though."

" Yes," he said, drawling the word and propping both hands behind his head again. " I can guess. The cemetery. I refused a big order from Levinsky a few weeks ago, Madge, because I didn't want the gossip to start; didn't want people to start saying my stand favouring Levinsky on the cemetery was tied in some way to family friendship. Now—I suppose the talk'll start anyway."

" Oh that," said Madge, with a tiny shake of her head. " *That* talk's been going on for months, John. I've managed to hear a little of it. About Jerrie and Frank. Even about your putting him to work in the store."

He was surprised, turned and looked at her. She wrinkled her nose. " Of course, love. Where have you been? Ask Miss Emily."

"I will," he said. "I'll do just exactly that. I hadn't heard any of it."

She smiled at him. "Well; I rather think people would be careful what they said around you. After all, you *do* have a short temper, John?"

"I? I have a short . . .?"

"For a New Englander you have. It only takes you a week to explode instead of a year."

CHAPTER SEVENTEEN

Some Changes

MISS EMILY agreed with Madge when John enquired the following morning about gossip. She said the talk had been going around for months concerning Jerrie and Frank and that actually most of it was reasonably close. That is, as far as Miss Emily could surmise the true state of affairs.

"What would this true state of affairs be Miss Emily?"

"They're going to get married, aren't they, Mister Leavitt? Well; that's what folks been saying. Is there anything wrong with that?"

John went out back to the loading-dock but almost at once one of his clerks, not Frank, came to tell him he was wanted on the telephone in the office.

It was Meyer Levinsky. He said, "Leavitt; I'd like a few words with you, but I don't suppose it'd be a good idea for us to meet at the store—would it?"

John said, "Down on the beach by Caleb's boat-landing. I'll be there in half an hour.

He felt mean about sneaking away to meet Levinsky as though they were conspirators but he was also interested in what the other man might have to say. It would doubtless include something about his daughter and Meyer Levinsky's son.

But he almost failed to keep the appointment. Charley Hudson marched in moments after John had rang off. Charley said, "John; Ed was to the house last night. Now I want to tell you that you and I're dead set on a collision course. You had no right to hint to Ed there was skulduggery afoot."

John grinned at the term. He hadn't heard it in years. "Explain away the speculators, Charley. Tell me they just happened to go over to the courthouse yesterday. Convince me you didn't tell them old Caleb's hundred acres along the river was a golden opportunity for subdividers."

"Caleb's land is pure business and you know it. Banks don't get rich making thousand-dollar loans to businessmen."

"And the other?"

Charley leaned on the counter, dropped his voice and said, "Levinsky isn't going to get to walk off with any nineteen-thousand-dollar profit, John just because we were all asleep, if I can do anything about it." Then Charley straightened us and said in a normal tone, " It's town land. It's hallowed ground."

John shook his head at the banker. " See you at the meeting tonight, Charley. I've got an appointment and I'm late now."

He left Hudson in the store looking after him.

The drive to Caleb's place didn't take a lot of time but by the time he arrived he could see Levinsky leaning upon the old dock, cigarette in mouth, gazing out over the broad, turgid Kanaki. He hastened forward to explain there'd been an interruption, then he apologised for being tardy. Levinsky shrugged, looking complacent. " It's a beautiful day," he said, and held out his hand. " First things first: The kids." He added nothing to that until they'd gripped hands, pumped once, then stood apart. " It didn't exactly shock us, Leavitt, but—well—my wife cried a little."

" So did mine."

Levinsky, always so sure and forthright, flipped his cigarette into the river and watched it sink before saying anything more. " That's got to take precedence," he said. " The other thing pales beside it—in my life, anyway."

John nodded. He'd followed all this without any explanations so far.

" Look, Leavitt; not much sense beatin' around the lousy bush is there? Well; we're Jews. You said it yourself. Frank? Well, Frank's some kind of misfit." Levinsky grinned. " More like *goyim*—gentiles—but like I told you one time, things change, times change, people change. Maybe that don't mean so much now. I'm willin' for it to be that way and those kids, they don't seem to even realise there's this difference."

"Then why make an issue of it, Mister Levinsky?"

Meyer stood gazing at John for a moment before he said, "Does emotion come easy to you?"

John shook his head.

"Me neither. John—my name is Meyer. It's a Yid name but I didn't have much to do about it. All right— John?"

"All right, Meyer."

Levinsky looked away then back again. "Good; now we're getting somewhere. Now about the kids—what do we do?"

"Nothing. They're both of age. They're both good kids. Frank's a worker."

"I didn't raise no bums, John. Jerrie—well—my wife loves her. And me; I'm not very good at expressing feelings out loud. She's wonderful, John. You know what I mean?"

"I think so."

"Okay. You got any objections; I mean any objections at all?"

John slowly shook his head. "I haven't."

Levinsky fished out a large folded paper and handed it to John. "Okay; this is backwards, I know. The boy isn't supposed to come with no dowry. But this is a peculiar case. Take it. It's my kid's dowry."

It was the deed to the cemetery. John held it and looked at Meyer Levinsky. "What am I supposed to do with it?"

"Tonight's the Selectmen's meeting. I'll be there. So will Frank. I want you to get up in front of all those people and say that damned deed is Frank Levinsky's present to the town of Newport."

" I thought you were going to make a fight of this, Meyer."

Levinsky held up both fists clenched, side by side. " You're lookin' at a man with handcuffs on, John. How the hell can I lean on a town where my kid—kid*s*, because this includes your daughter—are going to live? Listen; that deed is their peace offering to the town. You understand me?"

" Yes. Let me ask you one question, Meyer: Did you send some federal school inspectors round to look into Ed Smith's business?"

Levinsky slowly smiled and dropped his clenched fists. " Yeah. You said fight so I got ready to fight. I did a couple of other things too—like digging into the background of a couple of Hudson's friends, some city-boys up here to smell out a deal."

" I see; was a man named Staiger one of them?"

" Yeah; he had a prison record. So did the other one. The third guy was clean but when I went to their hotel last night and suggested they pull out, the third guy agreed to leave also."

" They're gone? But yesterday they—"

" Yesterday was yesterday, John. Today is today. They're gone. Also, I put the bee on Smith. I had another little iron in the fire too. I transferred seventy thousand dollars to Hudson's bank last week, then day before yesterday I called for an audit of the bank on the grounds of gossip I'd heard." Levinsky shook his head. " I ain't heard any gossip, but I fight dirty when I have to. Those auditors ought to be showing up about today. They'll give

Hudson something to worry about besides trying to crucify that lousy kike Meyer Levinsky." Meyer quirked up his mouth in a mirthless smile. " Now it ends. Frank and Jerrie saw to that without even knowing they'd made it end. So—tonight you give that damned cemetery back to the town. Okay?"

John said, " Okay. But I think Charley Hudson's got something up his sleeve for the meeting so you'd better be sure and make it."

" I'll be there if I got to be pushed in on a wheelchair. John; one more thing—about Frank working in your store . . ."

" He's the best clerk I've ever had. I'm not going to let him go for you or anyone else, Meyer."

Levinsky hung fire a moment over whatever he'd meant to say, then he shrugged and genuinely smiled. " All right. It's only that he's got this writing bug. In my business I don't tolerate conflicting interests; a man can't do his best on one job if he's always moonin' around about some other job."

" In *my* business," said John, " I only ask an honest day's work. What the clerks do after hours is their business. So far Frank's done more than his share, so if he wants to write a book in his own time, more power to him. We've never had a creative artist in the Leavitt family. It might be very interesting."

Levinsky's eyes were sardonic. " Us neither," he said, " And I still think it's a bunch of baloney. A book-writer!"

" Are you going to make an issue of it, Meyer?"

" Me? Hell no. *I* think it's crazy, but all right, times change, people change; I'll never say a word."

John stuck out his hand. "Anything else?"

"No. Yes, of course, a hundred things, only right now I can't think of them."

They shook and John went back to his car feeling much better than he'd felt the night before when he and Madge, and all their nagging little anxieties, had been without any of the answers John now had. He forgot all about having their deed in his hand until he climbed into the car. Then, looking back down at Caleb's old landing, he saw that Meyer Levinsky was already striding sturdily towards his own place to the west of the rickety old division fence.

There was a call from Jeremy Benson to be returned when he got back to the store. Miss Emily also said there was a call from John's wife—only she said, "from Georgia" and he had to stop a second. No one ever called Madge by her first name. She'd been Madge even as a child although her first name was indeed Georgia. He decided to call her first, and when she answered he said, "Is this Georgia?"

Twenty years before they'd had a routine they went through about that. She paused a second, evidently remembering, then she said, "No; this is Virginia, but Alabama and Tennessee are here if I can't find Georgia," then she laughed. The laugh told him all he had to know anyway. Whatever was on her mind wasn't serious; or at least she wasn't worried about it.

"I'll take Georgia first," he smiled. "Then Virginia and Tennessee."

"John; Doctor Gordon called a while ago. He'd been down to see Caleb."

"Yes." John's levity vanished.

" He said Caleb's heart is enlarged and they're taking him over to the hospital. Caleb telephoned to tell Doctor Gordon he was having dizzy spells and had to sit down because he couldn't keep his balance. They sent an ambulance for him. Caleb told Doctor Gordon we were his closest kin."

John made some rapid mental calculations. He'd be unable to get to the hospital during visiting hours if he waited until after the meeting tonight, and if he left the store right now, picked up Madge and drove over, it would be too early for visiting hours. He said, " Madge; call and see if Doctor Gordon will arrange to let us see Cal now—within the next hour. I'll let Frank and Miss Emily close up and come home for you right now."

She agreed and rang off.

John turned slowly to meet Miss Emily's steady stare. " It's Caleb," he said gently. " They've had to take him to the hospital, Miss Emily."

Her stern visage softened. " Oh," she murmured. It was almost a sigh.

" Heart trouble."

She nodded, tightening her lips as though bracing for a physical blow.

" Madge and I'll run over. I'll tell you how he is in the morning. You and Frank can close up. All right?"

" Of course, Mister Leavitt. And if you think of it, you might tell Caleb . . ." she let it run off into a hard, choked kind of silence.

" I'll tell him," said John, and went after his hat and coat. " Don't worry now. Caleb's tough as a cod. We'll have him back in a few days."

He didn't believe it as he was saying it and although Miss Emily nodded it was apparent that she didn't believe it either.

It was late afternoon when John got back into the car, sat a moment looking up the street with a heavy heart, thinking that if Caleb left now, he would be the last of the oldtimers John had known all his life.

He smiled, remembering something Caleb had once irritably said when asked how old he was. " Why do folks always have to remind a man he's old? Why can't they just leave it be, like animals do? No horse or dog ever gets told every birthday he's old, so the horse an' dog go right on feeling young and thinkin' young until they die, but not folks; always some cussed thoughtless idiot around to remind you not to jump off a log or not to stand up too quick. Seems like *people* can't wait to shove a man down into his grave. How old am I? Just as dad-burned old as I feel—that's how old I am!"

John started the car and drove slowly homeward to pick up Madge. He couldn't rid himself of that funereal feeling, nor could he blot out the look in Miss Emily's eyes when he'd told her about Caleb.

CHAPTER EIGHTEEN

Selectmen's Meeting

THEY HAD old Caleb propped up in a bed that looked far too large for its frail burden. He'd been neatly shaved and shorn, but what made him most indignant was the bath two nurses—both female—had given him. As he told the good-natured cherubic Doctor Gordon, "It's unfair advantage they take of a person in this place, sending females to bathe a man. I'm no danged invalid."

Doctor Gordon had laughed. "Far from it, Mister Adams. Invalids are people who've given up. You're a long way from being an invalid."

But when John and Madge arrived, Doctor Gordon took them to his book-lined office, sat them down and said, "He's eighty if he's a minute; under these circumstances, all the other parts being equally as worn, I would imagine his heart won't be able to keep up the fight indefinitely."

John had asked how long and Doctor Gordon had given a vague answer. "No one can truly say. I might predict six months or a year and he might be dead tomorrow. There is no hope of recovery, really, once the heart is expanded out of shape. I've put him on glycerine pills and will take steps to thin the blood, but there isn't very much we can do, actually. I can hold out hope to you but I don't think that'd be fair or honest. By the way," Doctor Gordon grinned, " he didn't like it at all when two pretty young nurses bathed him. Did he ever marry?"

" No," said John. " Although I recall hearing some interesting stories about Uncle Cal when I was an eaves-dropping kid."

" Good," said Doctor Gordon, arising. " It's good he's had some colourful memories, because it seems to be that's about all existence is, sometimes, the storing up of memories to re-live in the end. Well; you'll excuse me, folks. Take as long as you like with him, but please re-assure him on anything he brings up that might excite or irritate him."

Caleb's hair had been neatly combed and parted when John and Madge walked in. He glowered, but only until he recognised them, then his face brightened perceptibly. " I thought you'd be those girls again. I tell you, John, if I'd known all the routine they subject a person to I'd never have called them to come fetch me."

Madge straightened the old man's blankets and white coverlet. " You look wonderful," she said. Cal eyed her suspiciously, but she'd meant it.

" They might do a man a little good," he conceded. " The food's not bad." He chuckled. " Of course after eating my own cooking for fifty, sixty years boiled whelp'd taste decent." He studied their faces with shrewd eyes. " John; I wrote that out on a slip of paper last night —that thing we talked of the other night when you drove me home." He fished the paper from a nightstand drawer. " Take it. Don't read it now—not here. Bad enough to lie here without having a wake held before I'm dead."

At Madge's look of agony Cal said, " Pshaw, child; it was just a figure of speech, more or less." He watched John pocket the piece of paper and sighed with evident relief.

" Tell me something, Madge-girl: Are they really going to be married?"

Madge looked briefly at John before nodding. " I think so, Uncle Cal. Jerrie told us last night. Frank also spoke to his parents."

The old man suddenly rubbed his palms together in candid delight. " Fine. That's just fine. I wanted to know that. You see, for several years now I've been watching them. Didn't want to fade out before I knew. It'd be a little like watching one of those continued motion picture serials and never getting to see the finish."

John arose and looked at his watch. He'd just be able to make it to the meeting if they left now. " Caleb; you take care. We'll be over tomorrow evening at the regular time, and meanwhile if you need anything call Madge at home or me at the store."

The old man lifted a frail, white hand. His grip was deliberately firm. " I'll do that, son," he smiled. " Madge; there's a deposit-box at the bank with some junk in it. Nothing of any value but family stuff. You're the only kin left so maybe you'd better go get that junk and keep it at home."

She nodded, knelt to kiss the transparent old cheek, then turned and passed out the door John was holding open for her. Afterwards, John threw old Caleb a roguish wink and said, " Miss Emily said to tell you—get well fast or she'll be over here with a switch to pry you loose from all these young nurses."

They laughed and John departed.

The ride back was a gloomy one. Madge blew her nose with un-ladylike gusto and said, " He never looked so frail before, John. In that white room, in that big bed, he looked—small and so alone."

John didn't say anything for a long while. Not until they were cruising down the lighted main thoroughfare towards the building where the meeting was to take place.

" He's well past eighty, love. My father died at sixty-nine. Yours died the following year. Caleb's had a full life according to his wants and desires. I hope for him it won't mean lying in that hospital for a year or two withering away."

She alighted after he'd parked the car, saw Jerrie and Frank and smiled at them. They were going up the stairs in the midst of a sober-faced crowd of other people. She turned as John came up and said, " I'll go down and clean the house for him tomorrow—in case he comes home soon."

Upstairs, the chamber was already filled and the meeting hadn't begun yet. There would be late-comers too, but it was quickly apparent that there'd be no seats.

Charley and Ed looked up as John stepped past the little swinging panel that granted access to the inner area, nodded stonily and returned to considering some papers on the shiny big table. When John sat down Charley looked steadily at him.

" Fight tonight," he muttered. " Too bad, John. I wanted to avoid it."

" I'm sorry too, Charley." Then John smiled. " Well; we used to fight in school, didn't we?"

Hudson didn't smile at all. " What's a bloody nose

to a kid, compared to what can happen to older men?"

John brought forth the folded deed, lay it beside the lined tablet in front of him and said, " You've got time to reconsider, Charley."

" So have you."

John's smile winked out. He ran a slow look at Ed and said, " All right; let's bring the meeting to order and get on with it. Agreed?"

Ed nodded. He was pale and fidgety. From time to time he looked at Charley but the banker was back studying papers again and ignored Ed.

The spectators made a constant buzz of sound until John banged the table, called the meeting to order, then read off the Minutes of the previous meeting. There was no unfinished business to go over first, so he allowed a weighty silence to ensue, then brought the topic uppermost in every mind to the attention of his fellow Selectmen.

" The matter concerning the old church site," he said, looking at Ed again. " Mister Smith; at the last meeting you wanted more time."

Ed licked his lips. He shot Charley a look but the banker was hunched bulldog-like over his lined yellow tablet concentrating on some convulsions he'd doodled and did not look up.

" I been investigating things," began Ed, and paused, sounding a little breathless. " The town has a year to redeem the property providing it meets legal requirements such as cash payment, penalties and full restitution to the present owner."

No one uttered a word nor made a sound. It might have been that very wall of silence that unnerved the plumber but in any event he faltered, looking helplessly at Charley. Hudson was still absorbed in his artistry on the tablet.

John gave Ed a little help. " Are you proposing legal redemption, Ed?"

" Well . . ."

Charley spoke up in a deep, slow voice. " There is no money in the town treasury. If we redeem the property we'll have either to impose a new tax or borrow the money elsewhere against town receipts, and since the law is specific—this redemption must be accomplished by cash —it looks to me like a new tax wouldn't help us."

John sat back, waiting. He knew Charley was now ready to make his offer. Ed was enormously relieved and sank limply back into his chair.

Charley spoke on. " Even granting that a new tax would eventually meet the demand, we wouldn't have the collectable cash until the end of the year, so that'd leave us with the need for borrowing." Charley looked round. The packed seats held motionless, silent townsmen. He saw Meyer Levinsky, slid his glance past to where Frank and Jerrie sat together some little distance from Frank's father, then turned back towards John and said, " The bank cannot at this time advance the money."

John, impassive and relaxed, began to see the course Charley was taking but nothing at all showed on his face nor in his eyes.

" Therefore we must go to outside sources for the cash. I've taken the liberty of enquiring round to see who'd advance the funds. There are a number of lending institutions down in the city who could be approached.

There is one concern in particular that deals almost exclusively in community loans and bonds. They would advance the cash against the property, and at the end of the year it would all fall due—plus six and a half per cent interest."

Charley looked round again as though expecting questions. There was none forthcoming. Evidently the spectators were going to wait a bit, until all this had been threshed out a little further, before interjecting their questions and suggestions. Meyer Levinsky, in compliance with a fire department ordinance prominently quoted in black upon a sign over the main entrance against smoking, was chewing an unlit cigar. He and Charley exchanged a tough, unrelenting look.

John said, " Charley; if we don't impose the new tax where will the money come from at the end of the year to pay this loan off?"

Hudson was nonchalant about that. " I don't see any problem there, John. Not at this time anyway. If the town treasury doesn't have the money the bank will be able to supply it, I'm sure."

John bleakly smiled. " Is that a guarantee, Charley? If the bank can't make a loan now of no more than a thousand or two thousand dollars, what assurance does the town have it'll be able to do any better at the end of the year—with six months already gone?"

Charley's eyes slitted a little. " It still wouldn't hurt us, John. Even at the worst we'd simply have to pay interest and have the loan renewed for another year."

John slowly shook his head. " I don't think so," he said so softly the spectators had to lean to hear. " I think that the way the law is written, Charley, that if we don't

redeem that land this year—within the next six months—
we'll lose it forever."

" How?" challenged the banker.

" Simple, Charley; if your friends in the city refuse to
renew the loan, if the bank can't bail us out either, we
lose the land on forfeit to the loan company, and the
redemption period will be over. Someone else will own
that land and the town won't have a thing to say about
it."

From back by the door Jeremy Benson stood up.
" That's right," he called. " You either redeem it this year
or lose it for ever."

Charley Hudson tapped the table with a pencil and
kept looking at John. He was furious. His neck was red
and his eyes were like ice. John had seen through his
scheme too easily. Charley turned a slow, assessing look
at Ed, but the plumber, understanding the cold question
behind that look, began to shake his head feebly as though
implying he hadn't had a hand in John's ability to smell
out the scheme.

But Charley wasn't a quitter. He said, " All right; then
suppose *you* come up with a better idea, John."

The silence settled again, taut and drawn out. John
let it run on purposely. He felt cold inside. He was
ordinarily a compassionate man but right this minute he
despised Charley Hudson for what he'd tried to do—get
hold of that piece of property by default at the end of
the year when it couldn't under the law be redeemed, so
he was slow at picking up the folded, crisp document
lying in front of him on the table.

He said, " Even if we controlled that land, we'd still
have to face up to the need to move the cemetery. It can't

stay where it is—right in the centre of town with buildings going up all around it, with no parking place for folks wanting to visit it, too small for more graves, too poorly located for quiet and serenity. So if we owned it, still with our empty treasury, we'd still have to face the cost of moving the graves."

"We could get a loan to cover that," said Charley.

John nodded. "If we can't pay off one loan how could we pay off two?"

Ed was out of it. The dispute had settled into a restrained exchange between the banker and storekeeper. Hudson was bitter and dogged.

CHAPTER NINETEEN

Death Arrives

JOHN HAD no idea whether the crowd beyond the railing was with him or against him, but he *did* know there'd been enough resentment for the re-call petition to be in circulation, so he made his points concisely, clearly and firmly, believing that, recalled or not, he owed it to himself first, to the community second, to see that he was true to his own principles.

It was also clear why Charley had wanted him at this meeting. Without him Charley wouldn't have had his quorum, the whole thing would have had to have been postponed, and perhaps Charley's city-bred fellow-conspirators, who'd hatched the plot to gain title to the land, were impatient.

Of course there was John's ace-in-the-hole. He was holding it in his hand at the moment. It would forever doom the banker's scheme but he wasn't feeling like helping Charley Hudson salvage his respect and standing in the community right at this time. He was instead perfectly willing to give the banker all the rope he needed to hang himself, which ordinarily wasn't John's way at all.

Then Hudson turned slowly in his chair looked round at the spectators and said, " Folks; unless some of you want to cough up several thousand out of pocket to help Newport redeem the hallowed ground where those graves lie, I can see only one way out for us all. Borrow the money from outsiders, pledge tax revenue to repay within a year, and save our cemetery."

When Charley went silent John stood up, looked straight at Meyer Levinsky and said, " Folks; you've heard my views on that. I'll tell you in a few words where the threat lies; if we can't meet the loan at the end of the year the loan-sharks foreclose and take the land. The town treasury has been scraping bottom for five years just to meet city needs. There is no reason to believe this will change by the end of this current year. So—we'd lose the cemetery—and—I'm sure Charley knows that even better than I do."

Charley was on his feet in a flash, face red, fists

clenched. " Are you implying this is all a plot?"

John looked him squarely in the eye. " I am," he rasped. " And if you like I'll prove it."

" How? And by God you'd better make it good!"

John teetered on the balance of anger for a moment, then turned back to the crowded room, where everyone was sitting on the edge of the chairs scarcely breathing, scarcely moving at all. He held up the folded paper in his hand. " I don't have to prove it," he said ignoring Hudson. " This is the deed to the cemetery. It has been presented to the town of Newport by—the Levinskys. By Frank and Meyer Levinsky as a gift. We don't have to borrow money to redeem the land. We don't have to walk like blind mice into something that would in the end give title to some valuable real estate to outside promoters— which is what Charley Hudson's willing loan-sharks are."

Hudson bent across the table swiftly as though to swing. Meyer Levinsky stood up, his voice flat. " Wait a minute, Hudson. If you want to hit somebody let me say a couple of words then maybe you'll want to hit me. In the first place, I never once intended to make a big profit off that land. I didn't even tell my family this, but what I had in mind was to build the coffee-house and give it to my son Frank as a gift. Now, as a wedding gift, so's he'd have something of his own in this damned town. In the second place, I didn't want to cause no feud over the cemetery. That's why I bought three other parcels farther out and offered to move the graves at my own expense. And lastly, Hudson, those friends of yours are crooks. Don't look at me like that. I had 'em investigated. Two had prison records. I gave 'em a choice last night in their hotel room—stick around and play footsie with you setting up a fake loan business to get title to that land, or get the hell out of Newport and never come back. If they left, that would be the end of it as far as I was concerned. If they stayed, I solemnly promised to spend fifty thousand dollars, if I had to, bringing to light every shady deal they'd made for the past twenty years.

"Now Mister Hudson, if you want to swing on somebody, here I am. Only I got to tell you; I grew up where we learnt how to look after ourselves real early, and I'll bust your jaw for you."

Levinsky, still with the unlit cigar clenched in his teeth, turned away from the Selectmen and glared at the townsmen. "I and my son give you back your cemetery free. No strings attached at all. Take it. Don't even mention paying me back what I got in it. I don't want any of your money. Take it! And you've got to move the graves. All right. You can still have your pick of those pieces of better land I own farther out. Frank and I'll still stand the cost of moving and re-settling the graves. Still no strings attached. Stick that in your damned Yankee pipes and smoke it! Hudson there doesn't like a guy named Levinsky—a lousy kike—maybe most of you don't either. So think of that every time you go out to the new cemetery and decorate the graves. But Levinsky won't be around; he'll be back in New York where you'll never have to see him again!"

When Meyer sat down there wasn't a sound. Even Charley Hudson, leaning with both hands upon the table, was looking at Levinsky without offering to utter a word, and that was when Emil Franzen entered the chamber looking distraught, his cap in one hand, a slip of paper in the other hand. He whispered a question to Jeremy Benson back by the door in a low voice, but in the silence he could have shouted, everyone heard him say: "Where's Mister Levinsky?"

Jeremy pointed and Emil began stepping on toes, bumping and pushing his way over until he stopped in front of Meyer, holding out the slip of paper. Levinsky, flashing-eyed and still upset, glared. "What's so important it can't wait?"

Old Emil's Adam's-apple bobbled. "This, sir," he mumbled. "I don't know what to say."

Levinsky took the paper, shifted his cigar and read. The colour drained out of his face. He dropped the cigar and leaned to hold the paper with both hands and re-read it. He arose, pushed past Franzen and headed for the door very unsteadily. People leaned to give him room. Frank, looking puzzled and anxious, got up to hasten after his father. Jeremy opened the door for them to pass outside.

John heard a terrible moan as the door closed and looked perplexedly over where Emil had sank into Meyer's vacated chair. Emil said, "His son. The other one. The older son was killed in Vietnam this morning."

Shocked faces turned left and right. Charley Hudson sat down again. Jerrie jumped up and ran out of the room with John helplessly watching her go. Ed Smith said in a tiny voice, "We got to adjourn. There's nothing else anyway—is there, Charley?"

Hudson, looking grey, said there was nothing further on the agenda.

John pronounced the meeting at an end and went heavily towards the door without anyone barring his way

F

until Jeremy Benson, opening the door, dropped a hand upon John's shoulder.

They said nothing though.

He stood outside in the cool night waiting for his wife. When she worked her way clear of the dark mass of deeply shocked and silent people, he took her arm and went to the car. She said, " John; I think I'd better go out to Levinskys'. I'll drop you off at home if you wish."

He nodded.

The house was dark, which meant Jerrie wasn't home, but then he hadn't expected her to be there, not tonight.

He was tired to the bone when he fumbled for their bottle of gin and made himself a strong Tom Collins in the kitchen with one weak overhead light on.

Why in the hell had old Emil come busting in at that precise moment with so terrible a piece of news; why hadn't he waited at least until after the meeting?

John shook his head and sipped. There was no proper time for something like that to hit a man. He recalled Meyer, youthful, brash, noisy, too confident and full of life. He finished the drink just as the telephone rang.

It was Madge. She said Jerrie was with her and she thought they'd better stay the night with Mrs. Levinsky. The blow had hit her terribly hard. He agreed and hung up, went half-way to the kitchen to make another drink and the telephone rang again.

He was expecting anyone but the man on the other end of the line. " Doctor Gordon here, Mister Leavitt. I'm terribly sorry to have to call you at this hour of the night, but Mister Adams died in his sleep fifteen minutes ago."

John didn't make the second drink. Instead he went out into the backyard, dropped into one of the chairs and gazed at the lopsided moon with a great depth of soft silence all around.

Of all the momentous and memorable days in his life, this one was destined forever after to stand out in his mind vividly, minute by minute, hour by hour, almost breath by breath.

If there was any consolation at all it might lie in the fact that he'd already been in shock when the doctor had called him.

He didn't think of Charley or Ed or what they'd try to do. He most certainly didn't think of his own part in guessing how Charley had tried to work his scheme to make a respectable pile of money; in revealing what kind of a man Hudson had been revealed to be before the entire community this night. He didn't think about himself at all.

Caleb was gone and something of Newport's early time was gone with him. Levinsky's tragedy brought back something he and Meyer had agreed upon—that change doesn't limit itself; that if Caleb's world was gone, so was John Leavitt's world, as well as Meyer Levinsky's world. There were no longer natives and 'summer people', there were just people. Just human beings.

A car stopped out front with a squeak of brakes. John heard without heeding. He didn't even get up and go see who it was. It wasn't necessary, because the man's hesitant silhouette came round the back and found him back there.

"It's Ed," said Smith in a small voice. "John: You all right?"

John laughed harshly. " All right? I'm all right, Ed. What do you want?"

" Well; I just left Charley's place. I told him I didn't want any further part in it. I told him—"

" Go home, Ed," said John dispassionately. " Go on home and forget the whole thing."

" Well; but Jeremy come by Charley's place and Jeremy's on the Board of Directors at the bank and—"

" You're not hurt, Ed. Just go the hell home and make peace with your own conscience. You're a sheep—you've never been a goat anyway, Ed. Someone once said you were a pretty good plumber. Go on home and *be* that. As for Jeremy, I'll hear it all when I feel more like listening than I do right now. Good night, Ed."

" Sure," muttered the plumber. " Well . . ."

" Good night."

" Yeah. Good night, John."

Moments later the car started, breaking the silence, then it swiftly moved out of the area, permitting the stillness to return.

The telephone rang again but John didn't even look towards the house.

" Well," he said aloud after a while. " Newport got a fair look at itself tonight. I wonder what folks are thinking as they look in their mirrors about now? Levinsky rubbed their noses in it. He gave them more than any damned one of them would have given each other or the city either. Then he gave them a lot more on top of that. Not to mention a son killed so they can sit in the chamberroom squabbling over silly, pointless, useless things they're too damned cheap to cough up a thousand dollars to keep. That hallowed ground of theirs."

The telephone rang again. He looked at his watch. It was nearly midnight. Where had the time gone? He let it ring this second time without moving too.

He remembered something and pulled the paper from a pocket old Caleb had handed him at the hospital some four or five hours earlier. He spread it out and scowled over the great oval loops of the words. The paper said Caleb wanted his body buried beside his parents and grandparents in the *new* cemetery, and Caleb went on to say he didn't care where it was, so long as he'd be with the others. But the last line was dagger-clear.

'A town's no place for dead folks to lie. They should lie among trees and grass and birds and blue skies. Put me in such a place because I want to know now, while I'm still alive, that's where I'll be. I never liked the town and I won't like it any better when I'm gone. John; if you want to, you see me buried proper in the new place, and let that serve as notice *one* New Englander's not ashamed to set a precedent.'

John smiled. "You'll set the precedent all right," he said aloud. "You never were one to hang back anyway. Cal. I'll see you get buried right and proper too. Don't worry about that."

CHAPTER TWENTY

Newport's Conscience

THEY HAD to go down and close Caleb's house, Madge had taken the blow about as John had; coming so close upon the heels of the other death, it hadn't shocked her so much.

They spent more than half a day at the old house. Caleb, like many old men, had lived almost a pack-rat's existence. He had a storeroom full of rotting old books, magazines and newspapers. There were shelves with pictures, mostly cut from magazines, which he'd evidently liked well enough to cut out and save. There were even two ancient saddles, his mother's side-saddle and his father's astride saddle, along with a complete set of fine-harness.

The house was gloomy and smelt musty, but when John said something about that Madge explained that it had smelled that way ever since she could remember. It had to be proximity to the river that made it smell like that. Other things, too, doubtless, but primarily the closeness to year-round water.

Later, they claimed Caleb's body, sent it to the funeral home up in Beaver Falls for preparation and made arrangements for the storage until something could be resolved respecting old Caleb's last resting place.

Madge went to the bank and opened Caleb's deposit box. The articles he'd referred to as ' junk ' turned out to be a tarnished collection of old jewellery, mostly gold and precious stones. She didn't bother with an appraisal right then but later, when the inheritance-taxmen moved in like the scavengers they were to assess everything in order to tax Caleb's estate, it turned out the jewellery was actually quite valuable.

But the Last Will and Testament in the deposit box was perhaps the most enlightening thing Madge found. It bequeathed everything Caleb Adams had at the time of his passing to ' Georgia—Madge—Leavitt '.

John kept pretty much to the office for the next few days, leaving the store to others. Frank didn't come in until the fourth day. He was pale and his normally quiet eyes were dark-ringed. He turned aside John's suggestion that perhaps he ought to take more time off with a simple statement.

" A thing like this doesn't get any easier if you brood with it. I'd prefer being busy."

People, John thought, watching Frank handle customers, are in the majority tactful enough, but there would always be those tactless few. John returned to the office. There was nothing he could do to shield Frank from the latter.

Miss Emily wore a black armband, something John hadn't seen people do in a long while. In his youth most people denoted mourning that way, but somewhere over the past decade or two, although he hadn't had much occasion to notice, they'd stopped wearing those armbands.

Miss Emily said very little about either death. Concerning the Levinskys' loss she only said, "Those poor, poor people. They tried so hard to fit in and folks wouldn't let them. I'm ashamed of all of us."

She had more to say about Caleb, after the shock wore off. "He was getting very old, Mister Leavitt, so I suppose we had to expect it, but that doesn't make the passing any easier for those of us as knew him all our lives. I, perhaps, knew him best when he was younger— back about the time of World War I. He was—well—he was my personal hero back then, going off to a foreign war and all."

She never did admit how close she'd come to marrying Caleb. About their close relationship a half century before she said, "He was a handsome man, Mister Leavitt, tall and straight and spare. Any lady'd have been proud to be bounden to him."

The third day after the town learnt of its dual loss, Jeremy Benson strolled into the store and asked John to step over to Rosie's and have a cup of coffee with him. John declined but took Jeremy into the office where the percolator merrily chirped and they had their coffee in private. Miss Emily had departed for the bank with the receipts, a daily ritual she'd observed for something like thirty years.

Old Benson was a forthright speaker. He looked and acted, and actually was, a genuine, typical New England Yankee. His first statement was, "Bank's directors voted to ask for Charley's resignation, John. I had to wrestle with myself about it. I've known Charley most of his life—barring the ten or so years he was down in the city after college. That must be where he learned his sharp practices. I'm more than just ashamed of what he tried to pull on us. I'm ashamed *for* him as much as at him."

"Does he know?" asked John.

"He knows. We had a special meeting last night with him sitting in. He didn't get mad. Seems like he's sort of listless the last few days—since the night at the meeting chambers. I haven't seen him mad since that night."

"You've got someone else in mind for his job?"

"Yes. But none of the directors think the new man'll accept the position."

John's brows lifted. "Why not? It pays good and has a lot of prestige connected with it."

Jeremy agreed then said, "Would you take it, John?"

The question could be taken two ways but Jeremy didn't look as though he were being euphemistic so John said, "Are you asking me?"

Benson nodded, sipped his black coffee and sighed as though he'd already got the denial, which he hadn't.

"I couldn't, Jeremy, you know that."

"Yes, I know it. So do the others, but you were named anyway."

"Of course I'm honoured, Jeremy, but what'd I do with the store?"

Jeremy reddened slightly and looked into his coffee cup while forming a sentence with great care. "The directors thought that maybe, now things are changing and all, John, and with you perhaps having a little free time—or maybe you *will* have some free time *soon*—that since you're too young to retire and—"

John caught the thread of Jeremy's thinking in a flash and while the attorney was still floundering he said, "Jeremy; they aren't even married. They haven't even

F*

officially announced their engagement yet."

" Well, I know, but . . ." Jeremy made a weak smile and faltered. " John; don't think we're sticking our noses into your business. It's only that you'd be natural for the bank. We all feel that way."

" I couldn't do it, Jeremy. Even if Frank was my son-in-law I couldn't hang an albatross around his neck."

" Albatross?" Benson's head shot up. " Why, John, you know very well this store's one of the most lucrative in Newport. Albatross? Why, what kind of a young man just starting out wouldn't thank God for the remainder of his life he'd fallen into something like this?"

" I think Frank is the kind who wouldn't," replied John, thinking of Frank's book and his writing aspirations. " I'm not going to try to run their lives, Jeremy, which means I'll stay here in the store. Thanks very much all the same."

John stood up, signifying the talk was at an end. Old Benson put aside his empty cup with a sad shrug. He'd tried. He hadn't really entertained much hope of success from the start but he'd done his best. As he turned he said, " Couple more things, John. One's that re-call petition. It's as dead as a dodo. I talked to Emil and a couple others who got it organised. They said they were withdrawing it."

John nodded, not very concerned.

" And the other thing—I've been plagued by telephone calls and visitors the past couple of days. Folks are coming out solidly in favour of Mister Levinsky's offer for a new cemetery. Not one dissenter has called me or stopped by the office." Benson made a face. " Of course it probably isn't entirely based on Mister Levinsky's tragedy. You know practical New Englanders as well as I do. It's based more on the practicality of the offer. No cost to the town."

John almost smiled. Jeremy didn't quite believe that was it, but, as he'd just said, New Englanders were practical folk. What he *hadn't* just said was that New Englanders were embarrassed by emotionalism in any form, so while they'd undoubtedly felt ashamed of themselves for their sentiments towards the Levinskys they'd never in God's world *say* so, but they'd *show* contriteness, and this was obviously how they were going to do it.

"I'll see Meyer as soon as I can, Jeremy. I'll bring him to your office and we can work out the details. I don't know how soon that'll be, of course—except that it'll have to be fairly soon otherwise we won't be able to move the graves until next summer; once the freeze comes we couldn't do any digging."

Benson approved. "My thinking exactly. I'll leave it up to you." The attorney went to the door on his way out, turned back and said, "I almost forgot; Ed and Emil and I, as members of the steering committee of the Citizens' Emergency Council, have voted you in as Newport's representative in this cemetery removal undertaking."

John was puzzled. "What is the Citizens' Emergency Council?"

"Well; it only formed day before yesterday. Seems folks got together and organised it because they have lost faith in *two* of the Selectmen." Jeremy made a little deprecating gesture. "You know how folks are, John; they may lose their heads for a while, but never for very long if the question becomes an issue between what's decent and what isn't."

After Jeremy left, John got himself another cup of coffee. Jeremy had mentioned the formation of this new group with a deliberate casualness, which again was the New England way; play down emergencies, minimise shame, dissent, emotionalism of any type. He smiled.

Miss Emily returned from the bank to say it was hot out. She got a cup of drinking water and took it back to her desk, got comfortable and looked at John.

" I just passed Mister Benson on the sidewalk," she said, giving Jeremy the same formal title she gave all men despite the fact that she had grown up with Jeremy Benson. " I suppose he told you about the new civic body, Mister Leavitt?"

" He did. Are you a member, Miss Emily?"

" I certainly am," she said with spirit. " I think it's time we had some changes in Newport."

John stared.

" That Selectman-system was good enough in our fathers' time, Mister Leavitt, but folks need better representation. This way we all vote on every issue."

John's eyes twinkled. " Miss Emily, that's heresy. We've had the Selectman-system since the Revolution."

" Mister Leavitt, maybe that's what's wrong with it. After all, we haven't had a Redcoat in this country in almost two hundred years. We've got to keep abreast of the times."

John went out into the store feeling better than he'd felt in days. There were customers throughout the gloomy old barn-like building, but two people in particular caught and held his attention. Frank and Jerrie were quietly conversing over by the new line of boat motors. He hadn't seen much of his daughter the past three days.

He saw Frank touch her hand surreptitiously and smile. That was something else he hadn't seen in three days— Frank's smile.

Ed Smith came in with a forced smile and a sheaf of papers in his hand. He marched straight over and handed the papers to John. "That stuff I need for the new school," he said, forcing his gaze to remain steady and direct. "I guess I should have left the order with you before, John. I—sure was a damned fool, wasn't I?"

John didn't agree nor disagree. He looked at the list of material. "Ed; why don't you let this wait a few days?" he said. "I think builders can work through one another and come up with a bigger discount dealing direct with wholesalers than I can get."

"Builders?" asked Ed.

John nodded. "Leave the list with me. I'll see what I can work out on it."

Ed was relieved. "I'd be obliged, John," he said, and moved from foot to foot wishing to say more but unable to think how to say it, so in the end he just bobbed his head and ducked back out of the crowded store.

Miss Emily came to the office door, caught his attention and beckoned. He went over. "Miss Madge says she'll be down shortly to take you to lunch, Mister Leavitt. It'll be a late lunch, but then, as I told her, you haven't eaten yet so it should be all right."

"It'll be fine," he assured her, took Ed's list and walked out back on to the quiet, shady old loading-dock where there was a little breeze coming in off the yonder sea.

He wondered how long he should wait before going to see Meyer Levinsky. He hadn't seen Mrs. Levinsky in weeks and that troubled him because he wasn't sure just how to handle that. Then, thinking of his wife, he knew she *had* been with Frank's mother; she'd be able to explain to him exactly how to act and what to say.

He looked at the brassy-hot sky beyond the overhang-roof and was very thankful for someone like Madge.

CHAPTER TWENTY-ONE

Just People

HE SAW Meyer Levinsky at Meyer's invitation. They met down at Caleb's boat-landing, but this time it was because they both wanted to meet there, not because either cared in the least what the townspeople thought.

Meyer looked slightly less starched and immaculate than usual. His eyes looked older too, but only his eyes. He had three rolled plans which he stretched out upon the old landing, placing stones at all four corners as he said, " There they are, John. The parcels of land I bought for the new cemetery. One hundred acres in the small one, closest in, two hundred in each of the other pieces."

John knew those sections of land, had hunted over

them as a youth. One in particular—the northernmost two-hundred-acre piece—was well-drained, sloping bench-land with great trees and easy access. He'd never thought of it as a possible cemetery-site, but years past he had wondered why someone didn't build a home up there overlooking the town, the sea, even the river. But he was tactful.

" Which one seems best to you, Meyer?"

Levinsky didn't hesitate. " That one you're looking at. It's big enough to last a long time. It's also located so roads can be cut to it with the least effort. Then there's the natural beauty of the place. Do you agree?"

John nodded.

Meyer lit a cigarette, blew smoke towards the still, turgid river and said, not looking back, " Well; the Levin-skys have a reason now for wanting the best piece for a cemetery, John. Our son will arrive in a few days. We've been informed of that by the Department of Defence."

John said nothing. It hadn't occurred to him they'd want Meyer Junior buried at Newport. In fact, if he'd thought about it at all, he'd have considered it highly unlikely.

Meyer looked at him. " Frank said that was what his brother would want. They were close—for brothers." Meyer made a heavy smile. " Brothers usually fight. Not Meyer and Frank. Not very often anyway, and never over anything serious."

" Fine boys," murmured John, and picked up the plan of the proposed cemetery, avoiding Meyer's eyes. He tried to get off the subject. " Meyer; you paid a lot of money for this piece of ground. I don't think you should just give it away like this."

"Don't you? Well, look at it this way. Aside from the fact that I've already said in public I'd give it away, I've got a selfish reason—now. If Meyer lies there, John, it's got to be the best cemetery around. It's got to be accessible to his mother and me—and Frank, of course. It's got to have trees and a view. Meyer liked Newport. He used to poke fun at it—and the natives—but he liked it very much. You understand, John?"

"I understand."

Meyer studied the ashes on the tip of his cigarette. "Take the plans back with you, John. Show 'em at the next town meeting. Let the people decide which piece they want. I know which one *we* want, but let's don't influence no one. After all, Newport's got to maintain this cemetery over the years and that'll cost something, you know. Let's let Newport's taxpayers make the choice. Okay?"

John said, "Okay." He rolled up the plans and tucked them under his arm. "Charley Hudson was sacked at the bank."

Meyer flicked his smoke out into the water without speaking until he'd watched the parabolic rise and fall. "He had it coming. I never could stand his kind, John. Hypocrites. I hate 'em. I can stand enemies better; honest, outright enemies. Hypocrites turn my stomach. He was crazy to think that he could pull that off. Even if you Selectmen'd voted his way I'd have come in at the end of the year if you couldn't repay the loan. Hudson got so greedy he got blind. He wasn't talking in terms of big money, otherwise he might have stood a chance."

"There's something else, Meyer. Folks formed a citizens' group to more or less replace the Selectmen-system."

Levinsky looked up. " I don't understand village politics. Never had to and never wanted to."

" Well; from here on big issues for the town'll be decided by referendums. Common elections."

" Sounds good. Will it work?"

" It'll work. And there's something else. Ed Smith left a bill of materials with me of things he'll need on that school job he bid on and got." John didn't finish because he saw the dark shadow pass across Meyer's face. He tried a fresh tack.

" Ed's a good plumber like I'm a good storekeeper. Like you're a good road-construction man. But Ed let Charley lead him by the nose until it was almost too late for him to get out. He the same as told me that the night of the last meeting."

Meyer nodded brusquely. " All right; you're apologising for Smith. What's it all about—this bill of materials?"

" Meyer; you're a big contractor in the city. I told Ed I was sure two contractors working together could beat any price I could give Ed by ordering direct from wholesalers."

Levinsky stood impassively eyeing John for a while before he said, " All right. You're bringing me back into the community. Is that it?"

" Not exactly. I'm trying to bring the community out *to you.*"

Meyer considered his shoes. " You should have been a rabbi, John. Forget I said that." He raised his head. " You win. I'll see Smith. You're also a lousy businessman; you could lose a lot of business driving contractors into each other's arms."

"I don't need the business as much as I need—well—something else."

Madge had told him to ask if he could see Meyer's wife so he now asked. Levinsky nodded. "You drive out tomorrow morning while I'm in town seeing Ed Smith. She's adjusting. Neither of us'll ever get used to it, John, but she's adjusting. It was the first three days that were terrible. That same doctor who took care of old Caleb—he should rest in peace—sedated her. John; you don't know how something like this is and I pray to God you never have to find out. I'm going to say this to you I wouldn't say to another soul on earth: it must be a lot easier to lose babies or little children although that too takes a piece out of your life, but when you raise a child, go through every phase, every achievement and disappointment, every heartache and triumph with him—God but it's hard later on. It makes you know how age can suddenly descend. I'm fifteen years older today than I was last week. I'm not using a figure of speech; I *feel* it. In the muscles and back and legs."

John let him get it all out, then reached and touched his arm, something New Englanders never did—touch one another in friendship or sympathy. "I'll see her in the morning. I can't say anything because there are no words. I know that." He smiled and dropped his hand. "There are two good things: Your wife has you, Frank has Jerrie."

"Yes, and I thank God in both cases."

John trudged back to the car, turned and headed for town. But he didn't go back to the store. He instead went home. Frank and Miss Emily would close up.

Madge was out back in her flowers. He laid out the

plans with rocks exactly as Levinsky had done and asked her which site she liked best for the new cemetery. He held his breath because her decision was important; he felt that most people would pick the same site his wife would like best.

She picked the same two-hundred-acre area John and Meyer had chosen.

He told her of his talk with Meyer. She went back to kneeling among her flowers, both hands encased in plastic gloves. She listened without interruption and afterwards nodded to herself as though everything he'd said had been exactly as it should have been. Then she spoke.

" Do you remember Caleb telling us of those three men coming to see him about his land?"

John remembered. He also remembered what had happened to those three men.

One of them called me from the city today, John. He said he had a syndicate very much interested in buying the old place."

She finished with the flowers, rocked back on her haunches and lifted her face to him. She looked almost like her daughter, certainly as pretty and sturdy.

" He was the one who *didn't* have a prison record, John."

" How do you know that?"

" He told me. He also told me he had no idea the other two *did* have records until Meyer told them to their faces what he knew about them—and ran them out of town."

John was willing to concede this man was probably honest. He sank into a chair beside the redwood barbecue table with the plans atop it.

" John; he offered two hundred and fifty thousand dollars for Caleb's place."

He was stunned. " A quarter of a million dollars? Madge, you didn't hear him correctly."

" I didn't think so either so I asked him to repeat it. A quarter of a million dollars was right, John."

" But that's—preposterous. There isn't an old homestead in all New England worth that."

" I didn't argue," murmured Madge, " but your reaction now is the same as mine was at first." Then she looked at her gloved hands, began pulling off the gloves and said, " I told him I'd let him know after we'd talked about it. John; I was wondering—would Jerrie and Frank like the Adams place as a wedding present?"

That caught him off-balance too. He hadn't considered anything like that and couldn't make so sudden a decision now. Finally he said, " There's no hurry is there?"

" None at all. As far as I'm concerned that old house and the trees and boat-landing can stand down there as long as I live, unchanged."

He thought, watching sunlight play across her curly hair, she was *more* attractive, not less attractive, now that she was fully mature. He had to come back to grapple with what they'd been talking about by making a real effort.

" Then suppose we just wait and see what develops. Or talk it over with Frank and Jerrie in a few weeks— after some other things are taken care of. Madge, right now I'm overwhelmed with things on my mind."

She got up. " Would you like some fresh lemonade?"

He would, so she headed for the house, leaving him to his thoughts.

It was ridiculous. A quarter of a million dollars for Caleb's scrubby old acreage down along the river. Of course the syndicate had in mind sub-dividing all that land, selling it off in small plots for more summer homes, and that very clearly meant that within another few years Newport would double in size again.

Madge returned with the lemonade, the sun sunk beyond New England's faraway hills, coolness came to the little serene place beneath their immense old backyard tree, and John tasted gin in his lemonade.

He winked and Madge winked back. " You looked tired enough to need it," she said.

" Meyer will be home next week, Madge. I've been thinking: Caleb wanted to be buried in the new cemetery. The Levinskys want Meyer buried there too."

" But the place is still just a woods, John, without even a decent road to it."

" That's what I've been thinking about. We can get someone with a grader to fix the old road. As for the rest of it—that can all come later. It just seemed to be symbolic—Caleb Adams, descendant of two U.S. Presidents, Meyer Levinsky, third-generation soldier killed on a battlefield . . ." He looked a trifle shyly at her.

She smiled into his eyes. " I remember telling my mother one time when we were both in school that you had a poet's soul, John. You really do have."

He raised his glass and embarrassedly drank it empty.

Lights came on around the neighbourhood, people drove into driveways or drove out of them, all the same sounds of a town crept into the yard where they sat. Good little safe, recognisable sounds.

" Caleb said he'd never liked Newport, Madge."

She gently shook her head. "He didn't mean it. Not really. What he meant was—a lot of the things we all grew up with didn't please him. But then within the past few days I've come to agree with some of that. Still, love, Newport *is* changing. I think within the past week it's changed more than most New England towns will change in the next fifty years. I certainly hope it has." She went over to bend down and kiss his cheek before heading for the house to prepare dinner. "New Englanders don't welcome change, John. You know that. But they're visionaries too, so they *will* change. With Newport it just suddenly became so very clear what we were. No one really liked what they saw, I don't imagine. We'll know whether I'm right or wrong the day of the funerals. We'll see how many people come up there, John, and how they look and what they say."

CHAPTER TWENTY-TWO

Newport's Choice

JOHN WANTED a public meeting at the chamber room above the bank and Jeremy promised to see that notices were inserted in the newspaper. John also wanted the agenda kept to a single theme and when he met with Emil and the other members of the Citizens' Committee's steering group to ask that, they unreservedly agreed.

He told Miss Emily what was on his mind at the office. She was still wearing the broad black armband on her sleeve. She agreed that he was perfectly justified.

Finally, the day Ed came to see him, which was several days after Ed had been visited at his plumbing shop by Meyer Levinsky, John put it straight out to Ed that unless he wanted to be the one elected Selectman for the town he'd better resign because John had just that very morning filed notice in the newspaper that he was also resigning. That same notice contained John's words of encouragement for the Citizens' Emergency Committee, but suggesting that the word 'emergency' be dropped, and the word 'progressive' be used in its stead.

Ed remained in the store only long enough to tell John he and Meyer Levinsky had got along exceptionally well because, as Ed said, "After all, we both make our living the same way. I can help him on some of his local jobs too."

Jeremy called the following morning before John'd even got time to look over the mail—neatly placed on his desk by Miss Emily every morning. Jeremy said Emil had offered to stand the full expense of running full-page copies of the three proposed new cemetery sites in the local newspaper, but that the publisher had turned Emil down saying he'd run the plans as a community service, along with what particulars John and Jeremy thought should be printed.

That night John didn't get home until almost ten o'clock. He'd been at the newspaper office from seven until nine-thirty. Before that, he'd met with the steering committee at Benson's office for two full hours. That latter meeting had been very productive. Two local men had agreed to take equipment out and open up roads to the cemetery sites so the people could visit each one before making up their minds and voting.

Jerrie and Frank were there when he got home and Madge had kept his supper warm in the oven. He saw his daughter's engagement ring before he kissed his wife but he didn't comment. That would be up to Jerrie and Frank.

He collapsed into a big chair and told them all of what had been accomplished on this one day. They were attentive. He then leaned back, waiting. Frank cleared his throat, shot Jerrie a swift look and got a nudge which John saw and affected not to see.

" We're engaged, Mister Leavitt," the tall youth said. " But we don't want to be too modern about it. I mean, Mrs. Leavitt was telling us before you got home how you went first and asked her parents . . ."

John wanted to smile but refrained. They were engaged, he'd said, which had been a statement of fact. Not put defiantly exactly, but stated as fact nonetheless. Then, in the next breath, they'd asked for his approval.

He said, " Frank; you're getting the second-best girl I've ever known. Madge . . . ?"

She smiled, reading his mind. " I already have four glasses chilling in the fridge." She left the room. For a moment there was an awkward silence but Jerrie broke it.

" We looked at a little house north of town today." She sounded so young and her look of appeal was so pleading.

John blinked twice, rapidly. " Fine. And what about the ceremony?"

They fidgeted over that too. " At the courthouse . . .?" murmured Jerrie.

" If you like," said her father. " You don't want it in one of the churches?"

Frank nodded. " *I* think it should be there."

John thought he understood his daughter's sentiments but he only said, " Fight it out between you."

Madge returned and they drank a solemn, self-conscious little toast before John asked if they'd been out to see Frank's parents. They hadn't, but they were going now, if John and Madge didn't mind their leaving so soon.

After they were gone Madge said she was tired and John trooped upstairs with her, neither of them having much left to say, although both lay awake in the darkness for a long while afterwards, with their sombre private thoughts.

The newspaper displays brought a prompt reaction. People left town over the next week-end in droves, going up to inspect the proposed cemetery-sites. The following Monday and Tuesday John was full of foreboding. He wanted so much to have that one site selected over the others.

The following Thursday was designated voting-day. Booths were set up in several places and, again, the turn-out was heavy. But it wasn't until Friday afternoon that Jeremy called John at the store to report.

" That big two-hundred-acre piece up the slope behind town won hands down, John. I voted for that one myself. Which one did you vote for?"

John sank back in his desk-chair as he said, " The same

one, Jeremy. Now we've to pick out two good sites and prepare two graves."

Benson agreed, saying briskly, " I'll take care of that myself. I'll call Mister Levinsky; they'll want to select Meyer Junior's place. What about Caleb?"

John could close his eyes and see every acre of that land. " There's a flat place overlooking the town and river, Jeremy. It has a big old sugar-pine behind it. Caleb would like that place, I'm sure."

When he replaced the telephone and turned, Miss Emily was blowing her nose lustily, something he'd never before seen her do. She usually retired for that function. He got two cups of coffee, placed one before her on the desk and took the other one over to his own desk.

" Ed Smith's resignation as Selectman was in today's paper," he said starting up a conversation on safe ground.

She nodded, fighting for her usual attitude of eminently practical toughness. " I saw it. Right below your resignation, Mister Leavitt. And of course that leaves the town without elected leaders except for maybe one or two people." She picked up her cup. " There's to be a meeting tomorrow night at the chamber rooms. You'd certainly be welcome if you'd care to attend. I think the steering committee has in mind doing something about that."

He shied clear. " No thanks, Miss Emily. I don't want any more public offices as long as I live."

" Well, Mister Leavitt," she snapped back, having now recaptured her normal posture. " Newport can't just run along like a headless snake, you know. There must be—"

" I'll suggest one name to you, Miss Emily. But only to you."

She made her disdaining little sniffing sound. " I know. You don't have to tell me. I've had the same name in mind all day." She drank more coffee and then set the cup aside half empty and picked up her pen to go back to work on the ledgers. " I just wonder if he'll accept, though."

" Probably not. He told me he knew nothing about small-town politics and didn't want to know about them."

" Small town! Newport will be one of the largest towns on the eastern seaboard one of these days. It'll need a tough-minded, sound man to lead it up to that point too."

John agreed, finished his coffee and walked out of the office. He didn't want to mention Mcyer himself; he didn't want it ever afterwards said that he'd been influential in electing another town official. He'd meant every word of it when he'd said that he personally never wanted to hold another public office as long as he lived.

But he *did* agree with Miss Emily. Newport, moving farther away from its venerable—and hidebound—past, would need a tough-minded, practical man to take the reins. One who *wasn't* a native in the sense that he'd always thought of himself as a native, and as Miss Emily, even Emil Franzen, thought of themselves as natives.

He located Frank out back supervising some unloading trucks and took over that chore. He told Frank to go get his parents, take them up to the new cemetery and help them select the site where they would bury Meyer.

When the unloading was finished he gave Miss Emily the checked-off manifests and returned to the store to tell one of the other clerks to be sure and lock up at quitting time, that he was going home.

He picked up Madge and drove down to Caleb's place where the river lapped at the crumbling old dock. They beached Caleb's old boat, turned it bottom-side up, then went over to the rotting porch and sat for a while quietly talking. She told him Meyer's coffin had arrived in town that morning. That Meyer had ordered it sent to the same funeral parlour over in Beaver Falls where Caleb lay. She also said she'd mentioned to Frank and Jerrie that the Adams place was theirs if they wanted it.

" They said they'd talk it over." She smiled. " You'd think they'd been married as long as we have, having to talk things over. Do you suppose children nowadays are more serious than we were, John?"

" They'd better be," he answered. " They aren't in-heriting much of a world from us, love. They'd surely better be." He looked at his watch. He was certain that by now the Levinskys had visited the new cemetery, had selected Meyer's resting place. " Come along," he said, " I want to go up and make certain Jeremy got the right spot for Caleb."

On the drive she softly said it was most unfortunate so many things had crowded down upon them all at once. She had in mind his having a talk with Frank. He looked at her.

" Whatever for?"

" Oh; working in the store, their future plans, his writing." She stopped suddenly. " I forgot to mention that he sent off his manuscript last week."

He hadn't known it had been finished, but then he hadn't really thought much about Frank's book either. " *To Face The Sun*. That's an ambiguous title, isn't it?"

She didn't think so. " I like it, John."

" It doesn't tell much about what's in the book, though."

" It's not supposed to." She smiled at him. " Did you have visions of someone standing on a beach just staring up at the sun?"

He smiled. " I suppose. Where did he get that title, I wonder?"

" Jerrie said he explained it to her. He said it was how he'd always felt. He'd never wanted to face cement or asphalt, he'd always wanted to live some place where he could face the sun. Like Newport. So, because his entire story is about Newport, he used that title."

She looked a little uncertain along towards the end of her explanation so he smiled broader. " Madge; we're not exactly creative-type people."

They got back to safer ground as he left the pavement and wound up towards a forested bench of loamy hill-side where prehistoric floods had levelled off a number of stairstep ledges.

They saw the dust from motor-graders far ahead. They also saw other automobiles making their ways up through the trees. He felt kindly towards those townsmen up ahead and reflected upon something Jeremy Benson had said; that people could be counted upon to do the wrong thing sometimes but never consistently to do something they knew inherently wasn't decent.

They left the car beneath a huge sugar-pine and walked down where a square, deep hole had been freshly dug. There were spades lying upon the overturned earth as though the diggers had recently departed and would shortly return.

" Exactly right," he said, looking down over the bright

little town, out over the grey curve of ocean, and to their right, the broad-mouthed opening where the river roiled seawater.

She agreed.

It was a pleasant spot. Farther back they saw where someone had driven four white stakes. He led the way up there. Several people were mutely standing there. They all nodded and John turned to look in the direction this other plot faced.

"Towards the river," Madge said quietly. "Overlooking Caleb's place and the Levinsky estate. That's as it should be, John."

He agreed.

Afterwards, with shadows forming, they joined the other cars wending back down towards town. Neither of them said much. It was a still and breathless evening, very rare in New England in the summertime. When they arrived home Madge went into the kitchen and John telephoned Jeremy to congratulate him on picking the right place for Caleb's grave.

Jeremy was blunt about that. "I grew up here too, remember. I knew that place maybe even better than you did. And by the way, there's to be a meeting at—"

"No, Jeremy. Thanks all the same, but that resignation in the paper today was my swan-song as a public official of *any* kind."

Jeremy accepted this, then said, "Miss Emily called on me this evening at home. She had a name to submit for nomination to one of the high offices in town." Jeremy paused as though debating whether to mention the name or not. In the end he didn't, but he said, "What do you think?"

" You know what I think, Jeremy. If Miss Emily made that suggestion she also told you I favoured it."

" And what will *he* think?"

" That, Jeremy, is something else again. Maybe it's too soon. I can't say. But I'd certainly see that he was nominated whether he accepts or not. If there's one thing Meyer's done for this community it's to haul us up short before we went too far and weren't ever able to find our way back."

" He'll get the nomination," said Benson. " You can bet money on that."

He rang off and joined Madge in the kitchen. Their big house was silent as a tomb. He sighed and said they'd have to get used to that silence. She smiled. " For a year or two, John. Then it'll start all over again." She held up a huge steak two inches thick and marbled with fat. " Like it?"

He looked past the steak into her eyes and said, " *Love* it!"